R.I.P. the media as we know it.

Dedicated to the Afflicted

Who Town
a novel

Susan Kirschbaum

WHO TOWN

The shoot—a dinner party of a hip crowd of twenty-somethings—had been scheduled in mid January, but the actual story was to be published two months later, at the end of March. On that bright January afternoon, a wind that felt like bone-chilled fingers seduced its way into the neck of Sarah's cashmere overcoat as she emerged from the steps of the subway station at Franklin Street in Tribeca.

The blocks, long stretches of unadorned cement, made Sarah think ahead to hot summer afternoons, to imagine smoke rolling up from the ground when the sun pickled the air like a salty furnace.

Winter now whipped the entire city forward to conquer what would come next. No matter the season, there was never time to determine what was precious, and you couldn't tell a garage door from an elevator lift. Both blanketed the entire area, a ten-block radius, with practical purpose. Sarah rang floor three inside the metal elevator and was delivered there in one upward swoosh. Like a rabbit hopping forward in haste, she rushed inside, immediately pulling out her pad to jot down her impressions. It was one of those industrial lofts that dotted the dusty blocks west of the Hudson River. At the turn of the Twentieth century, factory workers had filled these spaces, crammed in against their black sewing machines and button boxes. In poor times, these 2,500 square feet would have fit a couple hundred toiling for their daily bread. But today, they housed only Roxy, a five foot two whippet like creature who called herself an artist.

Most struggling artists, of course, no matter what genre—painter, sculptor, tee shirt designer, rapper, gold lame bag maker—

could only afford to live—often in couples or groups—in the Greenpoint or Williamsburg sections of Brooklyn, or in Queens. In rarer instances, they herded to the Lower East Side, with Chinese landlords who charged a little over a thousand dollars a month for a one bedroom in a tenement. In those cases, tenants could expect bipolar shower-heads that varied from dripping icicles to scalding flames. Roaches and rodents traveled extinct radiator pipes, brought forth by the heavy musk of day old fish at pavement storefronts.

Anything bigger than a walk in closet in the gloriously hip neighborhoods below 23rd Street in Chelsea, Gramercy, East Village, West Village, Soho, Nolita, and Tribeca—replete with cafes and designer boutiques—was not for struggling artists. This was the land of makeshift homes for yuppies with day jobs, rich kids, and celebrities.

At 25, Roxy had taken over the grand Tribeca loft. Her father, a real estate developer, had bought the building two years earlier and requested that Roxy move into one of the floors, to guard his investment. So Roxy settled in, close to a handful of five star restaurants and a dry cleaner who charged fifteen dollars a shirt.

Tribeca residents valued privacy above all other neighborhood residents in Manhattan. The area still served as asylum for actors with mood disorders, men who lived primarily uptown but wanted secondary spaces for sexual affairs, and occasionally real artists who earned work/living spaces on the cheap in the Eighties (the artists were allowed to stay as long as they could prove they actually created their art a few feet from where they boiled their eggs).

Save for the few artists in rent stabilized live/work spaces, most of Roxy's neighbors were paying rent of at least $8,000 a month for a loft. Roxy paid $0.

And for $0 rent the space was filled with extravagant family inheritances, the most noticeable being a large wooden dining table with twelve settings, which Roxy nicked personally with various knives, from pocket varieties to turkey carvers. When acquaintances stayed the night, which they often did, Roxy would ask them to carve their initials into a bare spot.

This rectangle behemoth scarred like a sacrificial slab, greeted the eyes immediately upon arrival. At the center of the table, patchouli incense smoked through a burner.

To the right of the table, in an area known to most as the living room, sat two facing brown suede sofas, each atop oriental floor throws of peacock blue and white swirl. Roxy had thrown Moroccan pillows on top and two cashmere blankets. The ashen holes of cigarettes put out beneath the covers marred the edges of seat cushions.

New Yorkers shopped the 26th Street flea market—two black tar lots in Chelsea, lined with old lamps, furniture and bric a brac, an authentic antique environment—often called Boho chic. But Roxy had taken her mother's couches from a Park Avenue showroom uptown, each couch averaging the base payment on a studio in downtown Manhattan and a Beidermeir dining set, inherited from her maternal grandparents—then abused them until they became practically unrecognizable.

Roxy's sculptures, all carved wooden stick figures, decorated with neon war paints and adorned in various fabrics from silk, iridescent beads, and leather, were often distinguishable miniatures of her. Even the male figures bore some quality attributable to Roxy, in features or stance. And on two wall shelves—each almost two feet across, situated behind the dining room carving table—several of them assumed various poses. A few stood, a couple sat cross-legged, two held onto their knees. Several adapted a hybrid pose of mini wrestlers, forearms intertwined, as if aimed to overthrow. But their chins were cocked in such a way that they hinted at planting a kiss on the other in any given moment.

A lacquered black Chinese screen—angled like an accordion—partially shielded the sleeping quarters from the dining area. And behind the partition, Roxy circled her bed, stopping every other step or so to examine it, while tilting her head from left to right, like a surveyor.

"Uh, hi," Roxy said to Sarah, "I'm sorry I didn't come out when I buzzed you in. I'm trying to arrange…" Her voice seemed to fade into the cushions.

"Why is your bed so high?" Sarah asked.

The mattress, an odd short square—separate from the mahogany headboard that arched over it—stood four feet tall and was covered in mismatched silk throws.

"It's Victorian. Dates back to 1870."

"Where's Lola?" asked Sarah.

Lola, an erotic film actress, was co-star of the shoot, and was nowhere to be seen.

"She locked herself in the bathroom. Lola likes to read on the toilet. She can stay in there for hours," Roxy said.

The doorway buzzer erupted like a noisy hornet, causing Roxy to drop some pillows to the ground. She slammed a red wall button to summon the garage door lift. A moment later it opened to three silver rolling racks—the wardrobe for the visuals that would accompany the story. The stylist stood behind a hanging purple boa, which hung like a cobra, threatening to strangle her tiny white neck.

When the stylist pushed the rolling racks forward, Sarah heard a snap. She glanced down and saw that the front wheel had rolled over one of Roxy's wooden statuettes, which Roxy had placed on each side of the elevator door. A decapitated oblong knob head with white and red threads jutting from its crown, rolled across the floor.

Roxy, starting to pull at her hair, walked out from behind the accordion wall.

"You know, those pieces are fragile." Her voice sounded trapped in a box.

"That's Effervescent."

"Who?" the stylist asked.

"Isn't it supposed to be a miniature version of you?" asked Sarah. Roxy tucked her chin.

"They say all art is inspired by self reflection. Each sculpture represents a particular mood, so I've named them accordingly: "Distressed, Malignant, Flamboyant…"

Lola emerged from the bathroom. Fat braided copper locks thinned the sides of her oval face. She pulled a fresh Parliament from the front pocket of her red sateen kimono, as she crept behind Roxy.

"Flamboyant was her positive phase." Lola's voice cracked. She sucked out two drags, and flung the cigarette onto Roxy's floor.

Roxy's eyes remained fixed on Effervescent's body, as it lay broken on the hardwood. It was now just a tiny red silk kimono with wooden toothpick legs. She knelt down and picked the beheaded body off the ground.

Roxy cradled the figurine in her left palm. The stylist began driving the racks to the far end of the oak table. She hurled some indigo jeans at Roxy's face. "Put these on," she commanded.

Still rocking the headless figurine in her palm, Roxy grabbed the jeans absentmindedly with her other hand. Sarah didn't feel that she had witnessed the destruction of valuable art but rather that she had watched a child crumble: the head of Roxy's favorite doll had been torn off. Sarah wanted to mend Effervescent, to pull Roxy behind her accordion wall and discuss how the doll could be fixed. She thought about rushing out unnoticed, to buy some industrial strength glue, the kind of salve could mold steel beams together and could be found at every corner deli, next to the hanging packs of Chinese vitamins and square gum that resembled tiny bathroom tiles.

But the stylist, whose plucked black brows knitted together like inverted Vs, impatiently waved Sarah over to the far end of the table, where a hair dresser and make up artist had set up a couple stools and portable tables. The stylist was dressing Lola.

"We're putting Lola in black Rockla jeans and a silver chain mail halter. Sarah what do you think? Does it fit the image you're trying to convey in this story?"

Sarah bit her lip. "Sure. Whatever works."

Sarah wanted to place all of Roxy's little images: Distressed, Malignant, Flamboyant, and even Effervescent—with a newly glued neck collar—on the oak dining table. But her thoughts were interrupted by the heavy swoosh of pulleys.

The ensuing thud announced the arrival of the lift. Like a vertical guillotine operating in reverse, its blades opened to the apartment and someone new stepped forward every few minutes. So Sarah consulted her list, checking off each one on her call sheet as she recognized them. Lola's slacker boyfriend, who looked like a mop topped rocker but collected empty beer bottles in a Brooklyn dive as a bar back, hoping to advance to bartender; a tee shirt designer/club promoter known only by an initial; a one time novelist who wrote a history of the punk movement that Roxy had met the week before; and a female model, who knew neither Lola nor Roxy but was added at the last minute because—according to the stylist—"She looks good."

Rick Five stepped out from the elevator blades and shuffled to the window overlooking Canal Street. He didn't glance at Sarah. His typical black Converse high tops—the rocker's original jump the stage shoe—led his way.

He cracked the window and lit up a cigarette, and the draft caused the hairs of Sarah's forearms to sprout goose bumps. The silver valve from the radiator behind the table had sprayed Sarah's forehead with a balmy steam just minutes before. Now the sudden gust drew her to Rick.

Rick leaned in so close to the twelve foot windows, it appeared as though he wanted to jump from one of them.

The pen slipped from Sarah's fingers. To her, of them all, Rick counted more than the others as famous, at least in a tangential sense. Sarah scribbled on her notepad "Son of Rock Star."

As a reporter, Sarah did not critique artistry. In fact, the paper discouraged her from delving too deeply. Sarah was always waiting for someone discerning to call her on it, to tell her the articles were nothing more than celebrity fantasies that she and her editor had cooked up. But no one ever did.

In the beginning, Sarah proudly considered herself an explorer, a social anthropologist, finding those with enough talent or style to crack the beau monde, those who were "other" than regular people.

But, after almost three years with the *Tribune*, Sarah's subjects reminded her of the fireflies she used to collect in a jar in her yard as a kid. All she did was net them. With a blunt knife, she'd punch holes in the lid, so the trapped insects could breathe while they danced in the container, illuminating her bedroom. And unless she set them free, they would fall to the bottom of the jar and die. Then, she'd flush them down the toilet and gather new ones.

The stylist pounded her tiny fist next to Sarah's notepad on the table. "If Lola and Roxy don't make the clothes pop from the page or generate the right image, we'll use the model in certain shots instead. And my objective is to shoot the clothes so they are recognizable or at least will be credited."

"Sarah, you understand this right?"

Sarah nodded.

"Put out the cigarettes!" The stylist shouted to Lola and the bar back. The bar back was cornering Lola on the hair and makeup chair set up between Rick's smoking window and the couches.

"The *Tribune* doesn't promote smoking," the stylist yelled.

The bar back stood preening in a chocolate brown leather jacket, pulling the silver zipper up and down before Lola, who watched his peek-a-boo pectorals and licked her bottom lip as her hair was teased into a golden bird's nest.

"But we all smoke," Lola said dryly.

With her second and third left fingers secured around a Parliament, she threw her newly ignited cigarette on the floor. Still flickering, its musty residue rose upwards.

"Hey, aren't you gay?" the punk novelist asked Lola.

Lola laughed. "When it suits me."

"Stop putting cigarettes out on my floor, bitch. That would suit me!" Roxy said. As she flew out from her closed bedroom area, she seemed newly revived.

Lola lifted herself from the stool and eyed the large Moroccan cushions the stylist had arranged in a circle on the floor. The tee shirt designer, novelist, and model already huddled their heads together—moving their pillows into a single rectangle—as they shared the novelist's headset.

"Check this out." The novelist pushed a button on his music player as he announced, "This is live, never before heard, search and destroy tunes from London glory days. You're absorbing the vibrations of pure unedited anarchy."

"Lemme hear," the model piped in.

Sarah noticed that Rick, still airing his cigarettes out the window, showed no interest in the claims. The novelist kept glancing at Rick, while sharing one headphone with the model. He finally relinquished the full head set to the girl.

The novelist took a few steps towards Rick, and then hesitated before he reached him. "Hey man, you got a cigarette?" he asked.

Rick threw one on the floor, just in front of the writer's shoe. Then he walked to the other side of the loft, away from where the bulk of them had assembled.

Roxy, now taking her place upon one of the prep stools, was having peach powder applied to her forehead.

Sarah scribbled the words "Imitation. False. Pretentious. Empty. Numb…" in her notebook. Above them all, she wrote the word "ANARCHY" all in caps.

The slacker boyfriend plopped down upon a cushion, tumbling off balance toward the floorboards and dragging Lola with him. He coughed. The stub of a brown crumpled joint escaped his grasp and fell into the middle of her jeans.

Lola and the boyfriend started to kiss.

"Lipstick!" shouted the stylist.

The photographer snapped a few preliminary shots, using the caterer as an initial test subject against his set lighting, which cast a shadow of tangerine that flickered around her hips. The caterer had tied the thick mass of her waist with an indigo apron, and she was the only woman in the room who wore a dress size bigger than a four. After she was dismissed, she hurried to the kitchen where she loaded a tray of cigar skinny spring rolls. Roxy's oven door creaked from the weight of her arms. The patchouli incense, an odor that pinched Sarah's nostrils like musk and sugar cane left to ferment in a test tube, now choked together with the pungent herbed oregano of the marijuana. But the cold air from Rick's open windows cut in intervals of freshness.

She noticed the sunlight peering from the cracked door of Roxy's bathroom, like a beckoning fateful beam. And she welcomed a solitary moment. But as Sarah opened the door under the sink to search for toilet paper, she saw that she wasn't alone. Effervescent's head was peeking out from the swabs of tissues in the trash bin.

Sarah scrubbed her hands with liquid soap and carefully picked up the tiny cranium, then dug in her bag to find a square white box. She usually kept paper clips and rubber bands in there. But now she emptied the contents into her shoulder bag, putting in their place Effervescent's head.

MYTHS

The evening after the shoot, Roxy left a message on Sarah's machine, inviting her to a bar around the corner from Roxy's apartment, a place called the "Sticks."

Sarah's first impulse had been to erase the message, rather than to cross professional lines by meeting subjects off duty. To do so risked her impartiality. If Sarah were honest with herself, the impulse had less to do with the paper's official line, crammed into her head since day one, and more to do with Sarah attempting to retain her own disguise and power over her subjects.

But lately, the stories, so focused on celebrity, were suffocating her. If intellectual analysis and nutrition were valued on scale, then her assignments for the *Tribune* would be equitable with drinking cornstarch straight from the bottle.

Sarah had shaped herself into a walking, talking, two dimensional image once she had arrived in New York. She had built her own transformation so carefully, she could sense what pulsated beneath the cover guise. And as much as Sarah wanted to hide her own skeletons, she preferred to hint at the humanity of her subjects in her articles, rather than glorify them blindly. Like cancer, the myths were killing her, one nerve at a time. Not that she could get so close to her prey in an afternoon photo shoot, but with Roxy she would try, for herself, just for the hell of it.

It took fifteen minutes for Sarah to find the "Sticks" since no sign dictated the entrance, which was down an alley, not far from Roxy's loft. Only the number 47 scratched in black on a door hinge identified the place. Inside, nothing hung on the walls.

Roxy had perched herself upon a stool. Tiny votive candles cast shadows that danced against the red stripes of her hair. Sarah took a seat next to her, picking at bits of hardened wax that formed into rash like red bumps along the bar's edge.

"What are you drinking?" Roxy asked, as she finished off a vodka tonic.

"I'll have a Merlot." Sarah said, "I'm sorry about your doll."

"You mean Effervescent?" Roxy asked.

Sarah nodded.

"Thanks," Roxy said, "but she's not a doll. She's a sculpture. All of my sculptures are like a small family to me, the one I create."

Sarah laughed a bit hoarsely as she opened her wallet to pay for the drinks.

"The booze is free." Roxy winked as she waved Sarah's bills away. "I always get free drinks here. A few shots in a magazine and they think you're famous."

Sarah thought how somewhere down the line, by the end of her first year with the *Tribune*, the tables had turned, and rich kids and outrageous dressers learned how to manipulate an increasingly pliable core of publications desperate for ersatz glamour. Sarah imagined nudging Roxy's vodka off the ledge. But she resisted the urge and thanked Roxy instead.

"How did you start sculpting?" she asked Roxy. "Are there artists in your family?"

"No way!" Roxy practically cackled. "I'm from Greenwich, Connecticut. Ever been there?"

Sarah shook her head and lifted the free glass of wine to her lips.

"Well, Greenwich is a complete god damn bore," Roxy said. "Nothing but manicured lawns and manicured people who smile all damn day. My work…" Roxy furrowed her brows as if she were deliberating something somber. "My work allows me to express what I see in those around me, rather than what they want me to believe about them. Which, I think is what you can do, Sarah… with the writing, I mean. Right?"

Roxy placed her drink on the bar and folded her hands together on the bar ledge. Sarah could feel her stomach churn as though two mounds of sand had been pushed together from each side of her lower abdomen.

"Well, in a way I can write what I see. Still, I'm required not to take sides. And then it's fashion, or at least fashionable, so things need to be presented in a certain light…"

Roxy grinned and Sarah felt as though the concrete floor under her own barstool was cracking apart, like a fault line of an earthquake. If she had wanted to win right there, she could have told Roxy point blank, "Nobody takes your art seriously. You are a joke."

But Sarah wanted to know Roxy's story. It was her training as much as her instinct. Did her over confidence come from having her own seed planted and tilled by her daddy, in safe expensive soil?

Roxy lifted her chin to her palms to cradle it and leaned forward, with her elbows upon her knees.

"Sarah, where did you grow up?"

"Outside of Philadelphia."

"The Main Line? My cousins live in Bryn Mawr. A big stone house with acres of trees. Did you grow up near Bryn Mawr?"

Sarah's lip lingered on the rim of the glass.

"Just down the road," she said.

"Brothers? Sisters?" Roxy asked.

Sarah shook her head. "Nope, just me and my parents."

"Still together?" Roxy asked.

Sarah nodded. She wanted to give as few details as possible. If Roxy learned of Sarah's origins, she would have expressed no interest in her. Sarah could feel Roxy's eyes take her in from the bottom of her stiletto to the tip of her turtleneck.

Sarah had grown up in a predominantly working class section of Philly, at the end of a highway. Before the wealthy verdant Main Line, where the suburbs began, indistinguishable twin homes sheltered manual laborers and their wives, women who bred children like rabbits and moved like linebackers.

"Well," Roxy chirped, "I've got two older sisters. And we used to visit my cousins at the Grasshopper Club. And I remember those days when the girls and their mothers wore matching pink and green plaid skirts and Izod polos. Did you go to the Grasshopper Club?"

A drop of wine escaped Sarah's mouth. She wiped it with the back of her hand. Sarah imagined pert girls in checked green kilts at the Grasshopper Club with their ponytails tied with bows of lace trim. They qualified as upper class goy, whose Republican fathers wore navy blazers, Republican fathers with their Mercedes Nazi cars.

"No we're Jews, so we weren't allowed in the Grasshopper Club," Sarah replied.

Roxy pursed her lips. "That's ridiculous. I'm sure that's over by now. What does your dad do?"

"Did," Sarah corrected. "He's retired."

"Okay what did he do, then?" Roxy smiled.

Sarah pictured her father, a college drop out. How he would return home sweaty, stale like yeast after a day on his mail route. She'd fume inside of the smell of him, the after effect, the proof of labor. She'd look at him narrowly, suspiciously from an angle across the kitchen table, hoping that if she stared long enough he'd transform into someone respectable. One of those Jews with the mansions on the golf holes, the way it should have been.

Who ever heard of a Jewish mailman anyway?

Sarah blinked at Roxy and she could feel the areas under her armpits moisten as she lied.

"My father works in investments... but he's retired now."

Roxy leaned back on her stool. She seemed relieved.

"Every winter my mother flees to Palm Beach for three months," Roxy jabbered. "December to early March like a bird going South. So sometimes I visit on weekends. But she's embarrassed at the tennis club. She's always screeching, "Ya know Rose, proper women don't dye their hair cherry red!"

"Rose?" Sarah asked.

"Yeah, that's my real name."

Roxy's fingers were now drumming the bar. "The Christian family calls me Rose. And at the club, my hair really sticks out if I wear all white. So I let my sisters go with mother. And they think I'm a freak anyway. So I try to stay at the pool inside the compound."

Roxy's face flushed. As she brushed the ruby strands sticking to her chin behind her left ear, her hair could barely be distinguished from her skin.

She took another sip of vodka.

"Yeah, I call our house the compound. Ten bedrooms and most of them stay empty unless mother invites other couples for the weekend. Sometimes we don't even know if my father comes home on Saturday nights."

"How's that?" Sarah asked, thinking how ten bedrooms would have easily housed three families where she had grown up.

"What?" Roxy wriggled in her seat. "You mean my dad not coming home on weekends?"

Sarah nodded.

"Well..." Roxy drummed her fingers faster on the bar. "He worked a lot on weekends. Business dinners at the club."

Roxy did not lift her head. She stared down at her hand, examining it as though attempting to identify the notes of a piano scale. "Sometimes, my father slept at the club if he drank too many martinis," she explained.

"I mean it was responsible of him to stay there rather than drive back to the compound that way." Roxy cocked one eyebrow toward Sarah. She appeared to require confirmation.

Sarah nodded, but she had nothing to offer since her father, like the steady mutt, always came home. Sarah's mother had even taken to calling her father the St. Bernard, since he proved so reliable, at least in the way he kept schedule.

"Do your parents go to Palm Beach?" Roxy asked.

Sarah thought about the shack her parents used to rent at the Jersey shore and the shabby upholstered pullout bed in the living room. If her father drank martinis, which he did not, there would have been nowhere to hide him.

And New Jersey was a far cry from Palm Beach, where dozen room mansions painted white or pale pink dotted the shore outside. In Palm Beach, the insides were decorated in two forms: Chintz, with gold leaf mirrors and oriental rugs or art deco, minimalist cubed furniture with metallic silver tables and mirrors. Given Roxy's own décor in Tribeca, Sarah imagined Roxy, or Rose's mom, to be more of a chintz lover.

"My father hates the heat. He's got a skin condition," Sarah lied. "So we didn't go to the beach."

Roxy frowned. "How unfortunate."

Palm Beach was for blue bloods, Sarah mused, and she was decidedly speckled.

"You know," Roxy spoke in a conciliatory tone. "I can only stomach Palm Beach for a few days. They don't appreciate true artists there. I create most of my work in my loft, when no one is around. The ocean doesn't inspire me."

"How unfortunate," Sarah muttered, mimicking Roxy's original judgment. Sarah did appreciate the ocean, in the sense that for her, no matter where it hit the coast, it represented a great equalizer of civilization. Her own childhood ocean skimmed Atlantic City, where families rented row homes, the most elaborate featuring two bedrooms , the required pull out couch, no view of the water, but the sounds of seagulls nearby.

Her father would take her shell collecting. They'd spend hours on one narrow strip of beach, staying until most of the bodies, which practically sat on each other's laps at noon, had dispersed. That's when they could claim it for their own.

"Each shell, like each human, is unique," her father used to tell her, "and you can be anything you want when you grow up, Sarah. Find your own beach."

Sarah looked at Roxy, who was now leaning closer, anticipating some explanation, tale, or line of questioning from Sarah. But Sarah noticed that they were the only ones left around the bar.

"Rox, I think it's time to go… I'd love to come by one day to watch you sculpt, see your process. You're not what I expected."

Sarah offered it politely. She doubted that Roxy would even consider allowing her to watch her sculpt, or that she had even set a so called creative process, beyond aggravating her parents. Roxy seemed surprised and pushed her skinny limbs forward, off the seat.

"Oh no?" she asked. "What did you expect?"

"I don't know," said Sarah. "Just something else."

Roxy's old Waspy money provided reason, enough for Sarah to dismiss her as upper class gentile toast spread with uniform predictable mayonnaise.

As Sarah pulled her overcoat from the back of her stool, it dawned on her that she envied Roxy because Roxy believed in her dolls, her own artistic myth, even if no one else truly considered them art. And somehow, to Sarah—who could not ally herself with her past nor the present she had constructed for herself—Roxy's loyalty to her miniatures validated Sarah's own interest in her.

Sarah didn't believe in the celebrities she anointed in the newspaper, but Roxy religiously supported her creations. Sarah hoped that Roxy could teach her the trick, because for Sarah, her own value—her job at the *Tribune*—had turned out no better than rote motions on a pop culture assembly line.

PROVENANCE

Sarah Rosen, now twenty-five years of age, spent her formative years on 7314 Strawberry Lane. If you added the digits of the address together, it came to a six, like the six pointed Star of David.

It fit the circumstance since the Rosens shared a garage with the twin house next door, which belonged to the Murray family. Mr. Murray—a government clerk—and his wife, a homemaker, bore ten children, five boys and five girls. The Murrays referred to the Rosens as "that Jew family next door." The Rosens weren't religious. They visited Sarah's grandmother or "Bubbe"—her father's mother—three times a year for Passover, Rosh Hashanah, or the Jewish New Year, and Yom Kippur, the Day of Atonement and fasting.

On Yom Kippur, when there was no holiday meal to distract them from services until after sundown, they would attend Bubbe's synagogue. While such lack of observance infused within Sarah a kind of laissez faire Jewish identity at best, the Murrays never let her forget.

They hid behind bushes on their side of the garage to ambush Sarah after school, all the while yelling "dirty kike" or "Christ killer." And they would trip her so she'd fall and bruise her arms in some way. Sometimes they grabbed the navy Keds off her feet and tied them to tree branches. Or, they would yank her hair then moon her, all of them turning at once, dropping their khakis to their white socks while they yelled, "Jew kiss my white ass."

One night in the Rosen's basement, when Sarah had turned thirteen, instead of a Bat Mitzvah, Sarah's dad taught her how to throw a punch to the center of the face. He used a long pillow, while counting, "One, two!" And on three Sarah hit until she could throw a fist without shaking.

The next week, when the smallest Murray boy spat on her, Sarah knocked him down, back into the hydrangea bush. He speckled the fat blue petals with blood trickling from his nose.

And he yelled, "Jesus Christ!"

Sarah replied, "He was a Jew you know," He walked away.

Sarah thanked her father for the boxing lessons, but then she asked him why they couldn't just move away.

"Sarah, you are a survivor," her father told her. "Doesn't it feel good to know that you can defend yourself?"

It didn't.

After drinks with Roxy, Sarah remembered all of it as she hailed a cab back to her small studio in the West Village. She considered how Roxy and Lola had saved her momentarily, at least professionally.

"More ideas, more ideas," her editor demanded, wagging her freelance contract like a prize.

Sarah had been discovered by accident. After an art benefit, at a bar off Bowery, her editor had noticed her outfit.

"Darling, that's Herve Leger isn't it?" the man cooed, waving her over.

She had bought the black body suit, criss crossed in front and a linen skirt that almost matched in color, at the Salvation Army.

The body suit and the skirt cost five dollars. She had both dry cleaned for a total of seven dollars, and combined them to resemble a Parisian look that she had ear marked in a magazine

Since she had turned fifteen, Sarah bought Italian and French fashion rags and clipped pages that attracted her. Sometimes the clothes drew her in. But more often it was the attitude of a model or the location of the shoot—a gothic spire by Giotto or rounded Barcelonan columns by Gaudi—a full image, always foreign, that intrigued her.

Sarah nodded to the editor. "Yes, it's Herve Leger."

"Fabulous honey. What do you do?"

"I'm a journalist. Well actually, I work in an office. I just graduated."

"Alright darling. From where?"

"State College, Pennsylvania. I went there on a full Liberal Arts scholarship."

"Well, I'm an editor at the *Tribune*..." Sarah recalled how she had bubbled inside at this revelation. It was as far from small town news as you could get. Politicians, corporate titans, and other media—the intellectual set—read the *Tribune*. She told him: "Well, I've studied political science and art in Paris and..."

"No honey, you're a fashion girl. I can see that! We need a reporter in the fashion department and you look the part," he told her, as he snatched a card from his billfold.

Until then, Sarah had kept fashion in her clip box. She had never gotten close enough to the so-called beautiful people to understand them, so they were new enough to attract her. And she enjoyed the prospect, to dissect, not only perfection—since her own origins were faulty—but those altered rare creatures who could pull off wearing garments shaped like antique perfume bottles.

"Will you call me on Monday?" the editor asked. "So we can meet about the job?"

"Of course."

She had been in the city for only four months and had been temping as a receptionist in a law office. And she was willing to write about garbage cans for the *Tribune*. Anything for the *Tribune*. Sarah had spent her college years focused on journalistic fantasies that she could wield public influence by penning stories. If she did well, no one would ever guess that she had birthed herself from nothing, having crawled from a cement parking lot shared with a hooligan family in Northwest Philadelphia.

And the big-necked boys at State College, the kind who pissed themselves in bed, didn't distract her. By then, Sarah had vowed that "her first" would be of her tribe.

At nineteen, she lost her virginity to an Israeli exchange student, a longhaired sabra who dared her to sleep with him after they smoked grass in her loft bed. He proposed marriage and she laughed at him when he got down on one knee and kissed the insides of her elbows.

During the semester the sabra remained, Sarah had learned how to make a man come. He treasured her as his American virgin, cradling her before they fell asleep at night and again, each morning, when the sun woke them by shooting spears through the dorm blinds.

For five months, she felt loved, and she maintained a certain affection for him. But, she could not surrender to him or to any man, not until she had built something for herself, independently. She left him to transfer her scholarship to Paris for a semester, to learn French.

"Eye on the prize," she always told herself. "Success trumps love." Sarah's editor at the *Tribune* was in his forties. To her, however, he manifested his own form of 1920's chic. His seersucker white and navy suits stood out among gray cubicles and gray expressions at the paper. Sarah had begun working with him at the Style desk a month after he discovered her in the bar. He hailed from plantation Virginia and used to joke, "Ya know I got here by Route 54," meaning *Studio 54*, the famed Seventies disco, where he had seduced the fashion designer of the moment, becoming a commodity of sorts.

Sarah realized that before pitching the dinner party story with Roxy and Lola, just a couple weeks before, she had slipped in his eyes.

"So Sarah, who do you have for us?" That was his normal opener.

He had taken her into one of the conference rooms, away from the buzz of reporters manning phones at various cubicles.

When he favored her, he'd book a table at the fancy Japanese restaurant across the street and they'd leisurely shoot ideas over sake. But that day, they sat catty corner in a musty square room with a rust colored rug that had seen better days.

"Well, I thought we could do a story on politics and fashion," Sarah offered. "How some designers are making protest shirts against censorship and war. There are even meditation groups."

She was testing him again.

"Ahem." He cleared his throat to interrupt her, "Sarah, this is way too serious. You know, we'd much rather do stories about escape, fantasy. There's enough hard news on the front page."

"But this isn't hard news," she countered. "It's social criticism through fashion."

"Sarah, no real fashion trends have come from social criticism. In fact, protest groups have traditionally exemplified anti-fashion. And even if some designers are making a few tee shirts for causes, it's not where the money is. Think fantasy, Sarah. How about a story on where designers are vacationing these days? Hmm?"

"Well then," she continued. "How about an article on rich social women who are fed up with seeing the same Gucci or Prada outfit in the windows of every city, whether it's Paris, Milan, London, New York? Women who are abandoning the big labels to hire private seamstresses? I have examples of at least five established socialites who…"

The editor firmly placed his pen on the table next to his long white reporter's pad. His mouth closed tightly to reveal neat lines at the sides where his lips met.

"Sarah, you're wasting my time."

He ducked his head close to her ear and whispered, "You know we can't run a story like that. These designers represent some of our biggest advertisers."

The sides of his mouth curved upwards.

"Yes, but this is the *Tribune*," she said.

"Doesn't matter." He raised his voice a bit then. "In fact, even more so why we can't do that. Not in today's marketplace. What else you got?"

"Well…" she began, not convinced. "There is this actress, who has starred in these sexually explicit indie films, the one who works with that director Jarrett K. Well, maybe this is too young for us."

"No. Go on. Youth always works," he said. "These days, the younger the better." He lifted his pen.

Sarah continued. "She and this sculptor throw these monthly dinner parties with other artists, some musicians. I've met them through a certain crowd. But I never thought…"

"Are you talking about that sculptor with the red and alabaster striped hair?" the editor asked. "The one who's always featured in the avant garde rags? I think we shot her in couture."

"Yes, that's her."

"Don't the two of them have this lesbian chic thing going on?"

"Well… in a way."

His lips reassumed a straight seriousness. He lifted the pen to his mouth.

"Go on."

"Well I could be a fly on the wall and write about the party, how they interact," Sarah suggested.

The editor started scribbling as he spoke out loud. "And we could include recipes, little columns on dress recommendations."

"Uh, sure," Sarah swallowed, "we can also dress them in Rockla jeans."

"You mean that line the rockers wear?"

"Yes, they've got a new women's line." The editor again firmly placed his pen next to his pad. His lips curled so far upward. They revealed his gleaming white teeth. He clasped his well manicured hands together to express his commitment. "Get close to them," he said. "Get as close as you can, Sarah. This could be the start of many stories on this scene. It's fresh, really fresh."

Sarah had bought herself another six months on contract, but she experienced no sense of triumph. She felt as though another string had hitched her to the puppeteer's handles. She was crumbling. The age of *Big Brother* had not arrived. It was worse, the age of Big Bull in neon lights.

FEAR

The blades of the elevator pulled apart and Roxy carefully stepped into her loft. Beams of moonlight cascaded like stage lights on her striped hair. She had a way of hunching forward that gave the impression of a small cowering fox.

She grabbed one heel of her black velvet boots and wrapped it under her armpit, then did the same with the other to avoid waking Lola. But as she tip toed around her Victorian bed in thin knee socks, Lola shot up from under the pink coverlet. Lola pulled the dangling tassel to the rice paper lamp, which stood on her side of the bed. The rice paper lamp was the only item that Roxy had actually purchased at the flea market and that's why Lola wanted it next to her.

"It's the only real thing in this junk shop," she had told Roxy.

Roxy felt that Lola expressed her affection for the cheap lamp from a sense of guilt for what she took. Lola crashed at Roxy's place when the bar back boyfriend disappeared, which occurred about every two weeks. She ate Roxy's Captain Crunch cereal in the mornings, and she allowed Roxy to take her out to expensive dinners at Nobu, the pricey Japanese restaurant down the block.

The pale yellow emanating through the lampshade, illuminated Lola's long sad face. She moved her mouth so that one cheek rose up as the other side of her face grimaced downward, a dramatic half scowl.

"So what was tonight's pleasure?" Lola asked. "Were you with that reporter from the *Tribune*?"

Roxy threw her pencil skirt on the floor, as well as her black lace top with the bell sleeves and grabbed a nightshirt with the words Palm Beach Golf Club scrolled in green. She just wanted to wipe off her mascara, go to sleep, and skip the honey how was your day routine.

But Lola was her wife to an extent. Lola served her well as a social companion, an art house figure. And Lola needed her, so she owed Lola an explanation.

"Yep," Roxy said.

Lola pushed herself up on her elbows, while Roxy wiped off her make up with a tissue.

"So?!" Lola asked. "How was she? Is she some kind of gossip freak? Or is she one of those holier than thou high brows? Because I really couldn't gauge her at the shoot."

"She's… quiet," Roxy answered.

"What does that mean?"

"She didn't ask me about you, how often we have sex, or how is it that I'm bisexual, or if I've slept with Rick, or if my dad really owns thirty buildings in New York…"

Roxy trailed off, staring at Lola who now reached under her pillow to pull out the pack of Parliaments she kept hidden there.

"Sounds to me like she's dead," Lola laughed, as she shook out a match with one hand and shoved the burnt bit back into the cigarette box.

"I mean," Roxy started, "I didn't want to give her a chance with that stuff so I asked her about her family, where she's from. But you know, it's weird Loles, she didn't even bring any of it up. She just wanted to talk about my art."

Roxy shivered as she got under the blanket next to Lola and she hugged her knees to her chin. A fear shot through Roxy that Sarah possessed some nugget of information from an art source, that Sarah would out her as an amateur at best.

Every other reporter Roxy had met—from the fashion editors at *Vogue* who snapped her for party shots to the tabloid hounds who wrote salacious bits about her relationship with Lola— practically salivated when they queried her.

"So, where's she from?" Lola asked, taking a languid drag.

"The Main Line, Pennsylvania, near Bryn Mawr, where my cousins grew up."

"You mean the preppy cousins from hell?" Lola asked.

"Yes," Roxy answered with a hiss. "Same thing, but they have their own clubs."

"Their own clubs?"

Lola laughed. When she looked amused, Roxy could see the chip on Lola's front tooth, which slanted diagonally, a little bit like a fang. "Yes. Jewish clubs," Roxy answered.

"Oh," Lola mimicked, as though Roxy had revealed some great truth.

Roxy squeezed Lola's free hand. Seeing the fang made Roxy want to kiss her. She knew Lola kept her mouth shut purposely so people wouldn't notice the imperfection.

"So, what's her deal?" Lola asked.

"Dunno," Roxy said.

Roxy knew that Sarah wrote for the *Tribune* and that the story would be out in a few months so it might be a good idea to keep Sarah close, especially if she hadn't yet impressed her and she were snooping around for an artistic angle. Roxy still had time to pique Sarah's curiosity, to weave Sarah into her web of influence.

Roxy pulled her knees to her chin again. The more she went over her drinks with Sarah in her mind, the more it bothered her that Sarah hadn't barraged her with social or sexual questions. Roxy knew the dinner party story was just a fashion set up. But Sarah acted like someone who didn't really need to know. It was as though Sarah already possessed all the information, which made Roxy feel out of control.

Lola had been holding the round ashtray—which she kept under the bed—in her lap as she smoked. She left the bed for a moment and opened the bathroom door to flush ashes down the toilet.

Roxy watched Lola as she bent over. She liked that Lola always wore a plain white night gown and thick socks to bed since her feet froze into ice bricks without them. And Lola braided her hair into two plaits each night, so she'd have waves in the morning, like some country school marm.

These eccentricities comforted Roxy.

"Shut the light, Loles," Roxy requested as Lola jumped back

up to the Victorian cushion.

Roxy turned to kiss Lola on the lips and then rolled back so that Lola could spoon her at the waist. Lola snuggled close to her neck, but Roxy remained stiff.

With the exception of the first night—when she took Lola home from a loft party and went down on her—spooning was all they ever did. That was a year ago, and Roxy thought about going down on Lola again that night, anything to distract her from her own mind. But, Lola quickly drifted off and Roxy went over Sarah's words repeatedly, "You're not what I expected."

THERAPY

"I'm stuck," Roxy said.

She said the same thing practically every week and it was the shrink's job to unstick her. And yet all he managed to do was to loosen her up a bit so she could make it to the end of the week without doing herself any bodily harm.

Her platform heels hung over the edge of the doctor's brown leather couch. She reclined in such a way, on a diagonal, that her head rested low on the cushion. Her feet were propped over the armrest. From where the doctor sat, just catty corner on a matching brown leather armchair, she had assumed a position as though she had broken her neck and could not rise.

Twilight dusted the city. Roxy peered just over the tips of her shoes to the view from Park and East 89th street. The lights were flickering off inside buildings so high that their concrete roofs seemed to pierce the clouds.

Roxy always booked the last appointment with her psychotherapist, at half past seven, every Monday evening. It was the only time she would venture uptown, beyond 23rd street.

"You just think you are stuck," the doctor said.

The couch and chair, to the left corner of the room, both faced five large rectangular windows, with the burgundy shades pulled back to the sides. Behind the furniture stood a twelve shelf mahogany bookcase filled with collections of Freud, Jung, and countless interpretive tomes on aberrant psychology.

"Doc, I haven't created anything in months," Roxy said. "And I'm scheduled to see a gallery in two weeks. I'm afraid..." She trailed off.

The doctor tapped the corner of his note pad with a pencil as though he were striking a metronome, tick, tock, tick, tock. It annoyed Roxy. "Yes," he said. "You're afraid?"

"I'm afraid they'll think I'm a joke. They didn't want to see me in the first place, but my father..."

"Yes," the doctor interjected. "Your father did what, Roxy?" His voice elevated. By the time he reached "what" he nearly bellowed.

Roxy started to kick the edge of the armrest with her right shoe, in time with the doctor's pencil metronome. He usually got aggressive with her. Left on her own Roxy would take all night to divulge and he was on a schedule. She used to keep him overtime in the beginning, four years ago, when she had just graduated from Rhode Island School of Design. But she realized that he had gotten sick of her hesitations. He had caught on to her tricks.

She gazed up at the books again. "My father called the gallery since he owns the building," she said. "The gallerist is looking to buy another space and my father said he might negotiate with him If he considered his daughter's sculpture."

"How do you know that the gallery didn't want to see you initially? Did you call them?" the doctor asked.

Roxy remained silent.

"No," she said finally. "But I lied. I told my father that they wouldn't take my calls."

"And Roxy," the doctor was tapping quicker now. "Why did you do that?"

She couldn't help feeling that doc laughed at her, but on some level she thought that she deserved to be ridiculed, that it was safe to be ridiculed in a doctor's office, rather than in public.

"Because, I'm lazy," she replied.

"Really?" asked the doctor, still tapping, "tick, tock, tick tock."

Roxy thought about Christmas dinner when she visited Palm Beach. Her father didn't come back all weekend, but he left her a credit card on the kitchen counter with a note scribbled:

Dear Little Rose,
Max out the card, buy yourself some paints or whatever you
desire.

Roxy saved the note and read "Buy yourself some paints" over and over again. Her father was the only one in the family to even mention her art, even in passing. Roxy's mother called it "a waste of time."

"What if I let him down?" Roxy asked.

"Let your father down?"

The doctor often repeated what she said, in an attempt to get her to elaborate.

"Roxy, what do you really think of your art? Why is it that you create?" he said.

Roxy stopped kicking the armrest and sat upwards. She clenched her hands into two tiny fists.

"Doc, you know damn well why I create, or why I carve."

Roxy started to cry, to bawl. The doctor stopped tapping his pad.

"It's a vehicle so I don't cut myself, that's all."

The doctor sighed and pushed his eyeglasses to the rim of his nose. Roxy detected the remnants of his citrus aftershave closing in on her as he moved forward.

"Yes, okay," he said.

"But how do you feel about what you create? How do you feel about your sculpture?"

Roxy couldn't separate the work from their origins. She thought about the last pieces she had fashioned, over a year ago, before she had become involved with Lola. She carved 'Dick' a male sculpture, in leather trousers and a black tee shirt, after sleeping with a famous married painter at an art fair in Miami. He had promised that they would resume the affair in the city

Not only did 'Dick' never call but, when he'd run into her at art benefits, he'd cross to the other side of the room. She splotched the groin area of wooden 'Dick' with red paint, so it looked like he bled from his privates. 'Malignant' was created a month after 'Dick'. 'Malignant' was based upon a curator who courted and represented only male artists. Roxy sat next to her at a dinner party and when Roxy excused herself to the bathroom, she heard the woman announce to the table that Roxy was a rich little whore who went after her gallery roster. Roxy carved deep lines into 'Malignant's' neck and dressed her in a cheap velvet robe.

'Effervescent' was born just after she had met Lola. At a loft party in Chinatown, she had spotted Lola's most magnificent head of strawberry blonde cascading down to the small of her back. She was wearing a floral prairie dress with combat boots, which made Roxy laugh since it opposed the image she had in her head of this porn star.

But Lola really wasn't considered a porn star in their scene, more of an interpreter. They used her voyeuristically, to explore sexually the situations no one else did. And there she was, huddled on a chair half her size smoking and looking up shyly at Roxy. Roxy, who rarely chose women, felt in that moment that she needed to possess her. She took Lola home and carved 'Effervescent' the next day.

The doctor was leaning forward with a tissue in his hand. Roxy snatched it, absentmindedly.

"How do you feel about the art you create?" he repeated.

"I can't separate myself from it," Roxy began. "It's like you're asking me what I think of myself."

"Well," he said. But his speech was halting. Roxy knew the bomb was about to drop, "Roxy, what do you think about yourself?"

"That… that…" Roxy stuttered. "That no one will take me seriously. That, without the sculpture, I'm invisible."

Roxy started to pull the tissue apart with her tiny fingers. She didn't want to meet the doctor's gaze, now heavily focused on her. She wanted him to tap his pad again, anything to divert his attention.

"Okay, this is what I'd like you to do, Roxy," Doc said. "Start with your father. Go back to the last time you created a piece, what month was that?"

Roxy tore some more tissue. "A year ago."

"Okay then. For each month of the year, try to remember the encounters you had with your father, phone conversations, emails, anything. Then fashion pieces based upon those emotions. That's how you can start this collection. Does that seem fair?"

Roxy was sure the shelves of books were about to fall upon her and knock her senseless.

"I'm not sure." Roxy started.

"Well," said the doctor in an upbeat manner. "Give it a try. It might help to get to the root of your motivations."

"It's Lola," Roxy said, surprised by her own words.

"What's Lola?" asked the doctor.

"I haven't created anything since Lola moved in."

"So do you want Lola to move out?"

Roxy shook her head no. Now, she couldn't even imagine her life without Lola. Lola had become like her child. Roxy monitored her, made sure she made it to her appointments, her press interviews. And when Lola was too messed up, Roxy would call with a good excuse. Or sometimes, in the case of the press, she'd show up herself and grant interviews on Lola's behalf.

"But if Lola's getting in the way of your real work, Roxy."

"No!" Roxy shouted, "She's not moving out!"

She looked up from the couch. The doctor dropped his pad and placed his hands on her elbows.

"Calm down Roxy. You have control here, not me."

He leaned close to her. His nose reminded her of a chunk of play dough, the kind she used to roll into fat little tubes in arts and crafts.

"Look, our session is done for today," he said. "Think about everything and try creating something new, based on your father, okay?"

It all sounded like clinical mumbo jumbo to Roxy as she walked past the secretary to the elevator. She punched the button to the ground floor and thought about asking Lola for a temporary leave.

Maybe she'd ask Lola to stay at the bar back's place in Brooklyn, just for a week or two, just long enough so that she could lock herself in the loft, before the gallery meeting. Just long enough, to make art.

REFUGEE ARTIFACTS

Lola had made a game of which of Roxy's possessions she'd require for her two week "expulsion" as she referred to it. She rummaged through Roxy's drawers in the bedroom. She pulled out a rock n' roll concert tee.

"Not that one!" Roxy screeched. It was the shirt she had taken from Rick, an original of his father playing some massive festival in the fields, near Stonehenge, on a UK tour, circa 1990.

"Maybe I should call Rick and ask him," Lola chuckled, revealing her fang tooth for an instant before shoving the tee back into the chest.

"Does Rick even know you have this?" Lola asked, while ransacking piles of black and pastel pullovers. She pulled out finely sewn Japanese silk shirts with necks that flowered into cabbage like blossoms. The cabbage necks were Roxy's favorites, along with her long sleeved lace couture bodices, all misleadingly rolled together.

It didn't interest Roxy to lay them in any special order to preserve them. She enjoyed surprising herself. On most days, she'd close her eyes and pick a shirt, as though fate had dictated her choice.

The only simple piece in the armoire was Rick's vintage tee and even that, a collector's item, could be resold for hundreds of dollars. The tiny blonde hairs on Roxy's neck prickled and she could feel the blood rise from her chest. She had borrowed the shirt from Rick when they had driven to his mother's place on the Cape last summer. She had offered to have it cleaned, then give it back. But she always found another reason to wear it to one party or another, specifically when Rick wasn't around.

For Roxy, the shirt represented history. It symbolized two things: a rare artifact of rock n'roll freedom and that she was close enough with Rick to possess it, even temporarily. It was material proof, a step in her own budding iconography. She was too afraid to take it to the cleaners, lest someone recognize its worth and steal it. So Roxy schlepped to Bigelow pharmacy in the West Village, "stocking elite brands since 1898"—to purchase special lingerie wash, made from French lavender petals.

And for the first time in her life, as well as each time after she wore it, she washed it herself in the sink. She would wring her delicate ivory fingers through the worn cotton until her palms shriveled pink. Then she would hang it over the tub to dry as she might have done with perishable antique lace.

"Take whatever you want with you to Brooklyn," Roxy said, still staring at the balled tee. "Anything but that."

"Okay then," Lola shouted and thrust open another drawer.

For a second Roxy hesitated. Perhaps Lola seemed too pleased; too eager to leave and join this bar back whom Roxy never liked, from the moment last summer when she and Lola had trampled into the Williamsburg dive where he cleaned up.

He had tripped over a rug when he collected their empty beer mugs, spilling residual foam around his fly. Lola had grabbed a bunch of napkins and proceeded to pat him dry. Boys mimicking 70's styles, all shagged hair and ripped up jeans, watched this spectacle, pretending to turn coincidentally in Lola's direction as she wiped. Roxy wanted to smack the bar back in the face for allowing her.

The buzzer made a sputtering noise.

"Too late, the idiot's here," Roxy murmured to herself and in that instant, found herself regretting her suggestion that Lola actually join him for two whole weeks, fourteen days and nights.

But Roxy reasoned with herself that Lola—after snuggling with her and hiding out in Tribeca—usually ended up at his place anyway.

Lola zipped the khaki duffel bag she had filled with Roxy's clothing and hit the wall buzzer to send the elevator down. Roxy had telephoned the bar back personally, to escort Lola, and to carry her overnight bags out to the car she had hired. Ordinarily, Lola would have thrown a few items into a duffel, and taken the L train to Williamsburg, no pickups necessary. But Roxy had hired a limo service, charged to her father's account, to take them back to the hovel he shared with two other guys. Roxy felt that by offering this service, and by his acceptance, it indicated that she was leasing Lola out the same way she had leased the car: temporarily. Lola was to be returned in mint condition, without a scratch.

"Hey, Rox," the bar back nodded toward Roxy as she emerged from behind the accordion wall. "She ready?" he asked.

Before Roxy could answer, Lola came out, plopped the bag at her feet and pulled a Parliament from the back pocket of her blue jeans. Roxy nodded toward Lola's luggage, for the bar back to pick up. He obliged, turning his back, practically tripping over the laces of his Chucks, and stumbled into the lift. Roxy snatched Lola's cigarette with her right hand raising it into the air like some dramatic queen, while enveloping her left arm around Lola's waist. She kissed Lola full on the mouth, inserting her tongue hard into the back of her throat. Lola volleyed back, then pulled Roxy's hand off her waist.

"Hot!" She cackled and winked at Roxy.

"C'mon you dykes," the boy yelled. The elevator rang, a shrill bell that bleated every few seconds since he had held the floor for too long, meaning someone else in the building had already sent for it. Lola skipped toward the lift and like a beauty pageant contestant, waved in an exaggerated fashion to Roxy.

Now I can work. Roxy thought as she flushed Lola's cigarette, with the ashes piled up almost to the stub, down the toilet. Roxy circled around her space, at first aimlessly, picking up each sculpture, mentally ticking off the old repertoire. She hadn't been alone—truly alone—in so long. As she knelt on the hardwood planks to open the chest she kept under her shelves of sculptures behind the dining table, she was gripped with a fear that Lola might not return to her. It seemed as though a donut ring clamped her aorta. She reached for her tools.

She pulled out five carving knives of various sizes: a butcher knife which Roxy used when she wanted to rub the nubs of her fingers around a tool larger than her forearm, two medium sized shaving knives, one five, the other six inches in diameter, a long thin cutter with a shiny smooth handle, which she had purchased from a gentleman who carved birdbaths in Vermont and a pocket knife she bought with Rick in Harlem, true gang land style, with three blades that flipped back with each click of a miniscule knob at the base.

Roxy placed them on the table, then opened the tiniest gang knife in the three bladed switch. She ran her forefinger down the middle to test it, scratching a thin line that sprouted drops of blood. She lifted it just under her left shoulder and winced as it ripped through her flesh. She plunged it down and over, as though she were filleting a chicken breast, into the sharp curve of an "L."

The blood seemed to rush from her temples like the spin of two heavy wheels spiraling backwards, picking up pace, lighter and quicker by the second. This sensation caused Roxy to sway a bit from side to side, followed by spontaneous jolts.

Her eyes stung with delightful tears as her breath returned, steady, with vigor. Blood slipped down to her wrist and Roxy laughed a little.

She hastened to the bathroom since the blood now dripped in zigzag dots on the floor. Once she doused her wound and fashioned the bandage, the exorcism of her fear would be complete. With her unhindered arm, she opened the medicine cabinet and grabbed a plastic bottle of peroxide. The skin surrounding Roxy's mark had begun to swell, like one of those oblong balloons, and she knew she needed to just do it, to throw the peroxide into the air over her arm. So she counted, "one, two, …two …two." On three, the liquid flowed over her cut.

It was as through an entire side of her body had been lit with a torch. She could feel herself dropping, one limb at a time, to the cool relief of the bathroom tiles.

The hard icy surface eased her clammy soiled skin. She could feel herself drifting skyward in one minute, scorched steam rising from her body, then sinking as if being swallowed into hot bubbling mud, the next. She realized a fever had set in.

By the following morning, once the delirium had subsided, she'd begin to carve from blocks of wood. But first, she needed to exorcise her feelings. This was the only way she knew how to begin.

FOREIGN INVADERS

Rick rummaged through the pile of tees he had thrown into the chest, all of them his father's tour shirts, hundreds of them piled like heaps of garbage. He never wore them, but his weekly maid had gotten sick, so he was faced with a shortage of clean laundry.

Rick thought about pulling his own load, with a bottle of detergent, to the fancy basement laundry room lined with slick shiny washers. But no matter where he went, even in his own building, the doorman and his neighbors watched him.

He picked through each tour USA, Italy, Spain, Australia, New Zealand, France, and the UK. The UK tees always changed design with each city: London, Cornwall, Leeds, Manchester, Liverpool, Suffolk, and Stonehenge.

Rick had at least five shirts from each tour date, which spanned the Eighties, the early years of Rick's life, years he only saw his father on holidays. He thought about selling the shirts. But he couldn't allow himself, since they represented evidence of his actual childhood and proof that his dad wasn't there for it.

Stonehenge really irked him. It was at Stonehenge that his father had fucked the groupie behind one of the oracles and it became front-page news. It gave his father infamous rock cache. And it gave his mother infinite grief, since Rick clearly remembered the morning after the concert when the porter in their New York apartment handed Rick the global papers. The fucking porter had a ridiculous wide grin.

Rick, just ten, ambled toward the kitchen, without glancing

at the pages. His mother was poaching some eggbeaters with a spatula. When he handed her the pages, she nearly torched the room. It was the only time he needed to save his mother. He pulled her away from the burners which had burst into flames, the papers falling on to the fryer, spitting orange like a burning bush.

"No," he told himself. As he shut the lid on the tee shirt chest, he decided he'd rather wear a dirty Hanes than his father on his chest.

Rick had a half an hour before the gig. He and the guys, his crew, were set to open for some indie rockers from Sweden with pretty hair. Rick didn't want to do it. But as long as Rick asked his crew to sit out songs, to allow him to play his ballads, they'd pressure him to open for trendy groups.

"Good evening, Mr. Five." The doorman saluted him on the way out. The doorman's gray sideburns sprouted from his green captain's cap.

"Yes sir," Rick said, grinning.

He only did this because he and the doorman were alone. Most other times Rick would walk by as though he were deaf.

Rick had bought the apartment, a one bedroom on 13th between 2nd and 3rd, a couple years ago; when he had turned twenty-one and his mother had moved to Cape Cod. Before that, he spent his later teen years living with two of his crew since their fathers—all musicians—were on the road. Then, the crew had pix of Rick's father's band—metal rockers—on the back of their bedroom doors. On the back of Rick's door, however, hung a poster of Bob Dylan.

"Hey man!" Rick's bassist leaned against the bright cherry entrance to the concert space on Bowery. Accompanied by loud guitar riffs, which echoed like audible mammoth coils from the roof, the doors stood out. Rick found them amusing, as if they existed to prepare the children in the same way Disneyland featured bright colored ticket booths.

"No rush, now. The Swedes ain't here," the bassist said and hi-fived Rick.

They walked inside together.

The entire place—the bar area, located in the entrance

hallway, the first floor seats, and second floor balcony—smelled like piss, cigarettes, cheap licorice cologne, and pine spray air freshener.

Rick pulled out a silver cell phone from his back jeans pocket to check the time. It was fifteen minutes before their set. He heard the manager of the Bowery Hall complaining to a bartender about the Swedes, "Yeah, they're probably getting their hair straightened and their jeans sprayed on."

Rick remembered his initial hesitation about the show. He regretted that he shared a poster with some girly boys from Sweden.

His guys were not official. They had no name, just 'Rick Five's band' on the sign that evening. But they also didn't take themselves as seriously as the Swedes and should not have been paired with them.

If the mood agreed, Rick would invite the crew to jam, and they'd follow him, to one loft or another, often to Roxy's place. And since five of them played together: Rick on vocals and guitar, bass, a second guitar, drums, and portable keyboard, Roxy would call them "The Five Fuckers."

Rick and the bassist entered a side door. It led down graffiti and piss stained hallway, to the back stage area, which was just the stage hidden behind a material divider called a scrim.

The bassist handed Rick the electric guitar, which he had brought earlier in his van, and Rick plucked a few strings. He mimicked a Zeppelin riff but transposed the chords. He had learned guitar on his own from songbooks his dad kept laying around the apartment.

Rick's eyes darted around the equipment, boxed amplifiers, a glitter hued drum set, guitar cases.

"Hey, where's my acoustic?" he asked.

"Uh, it's still in the van. Ya know they're only giving us six songs," the bassist said, and shrugged his shoulders.

"What do you mean, it's still in the fucking van?" Rick screamed. He knew they didn't want him to use it, that they hated his poetry and behind his back they called it "strum hum."

The bassist laid his instrument against the wall. As he darted to the side door to get Ricks' acoustic guitar, the owner of the Bowery, a big burly guy with the face of a mutt, nearly knocked him down.

The Bowery owner stood before Rick, casting a shadow that hit well above Rick's shoulders. "You think you guys can make it last, like twelve, fifteen songs?" he asked Rick.

"Swedes bail?" Rick inquired.

"They're coming, but they're about an hour late. So, I need you to keep 'em entertained."

The owner walked back to the side door, then turned toward Rick. He placed his hand upon the knob before he exited.

"Hey, play some of your dad's songs," he said.

Rick's keyboardist practiced some scales and the drummer was just setting up, when the bassist returned with one of Rick's acoustics.

Besides this one, Rick owned four acoustic guitars, plus three electric—two used by his father—that he kept in his apartment.

"Did you tell him that we were some cover band?" Rick shouted at the bassist as he laid the acoustic down at Ricks' feet. "Did you?"

"No man," the other guitarist said from behind both of them. "We told him all original songs, our stuff."

Rick liked the music that he wrote and the crew played—ultimately derivative of their fathers' tunes—when they could serve it as an exaggerated parody, which is why Rick secretly appreciated Roxy's title "The Five Fuckers." That way, they played an inside joke among friends.

"But this was an actual gig, where people paid to see… To see… Fucking Swedes," Rick said as he leaned his acoustic against the wall and plucked at the electric again.

"Five minutes, guys," the Bowery owner announced, popping his head through the door. "Just keep playing until I give you the signal."

"What's the signal?" the keyboardist asked, but the door had already shut.

The opaque scrim went up.

Rick pinched his pick tightly between his thumb and forefinger. He could feel the tremors that pulsed through his arms. He didn't want the guys to detect any lapse of confidence. Thankfully, the guitar shielded him, since it stood three quarters his height.

The lights burned down on his skull, but he kept his leather jacket zippered from the waist to his neck, with the collar upward.

He had allowed his hair to grow outwards into a "fro" with crazy frizzy curls, like Dylan. As Rick looked out into the crowd, he counted on his guitar and his fro, as adequate barriers.

"Hey." He rasped into the mike, as if he were responding not to the elevated scrim, but to a woman who had hiked her skirt up, just for him. Hundreds of girls, and boys—who mimicked chicks with their skinny tight pants, shagged hair, and bangs—gazed at him silently. They wanted electro Swede and Rick was about to give them American.

Rick clutched his guitar so it pushed into his abdomen. He tapped his right foot twice, then raised his hand to give the signal to his crew.

The phrases burst out in jolts, which he pulled into smooth deep layers. Then he stopped, hit a few guitar cords, and began the chorus again:

You tried to trap me in your empty womb
But I never crawled in that far
There's nobody home, since I've been alone
And holding me won't heal your scar

Rick had written the song after he and Roxy spent a week at his mother's beach house the previous summer. She had inspired the lyrics. And they erupted so perfectly between the dueling guitar riffs of his bassist and second guitar, Rick felt like he would come any minute, right there on stage.

His knees were buckling under his instrument, as he charged toward the finish.

They lied to you when they said that
Daddy was mending Cause Daddy just don't care
So as soon as you know that nobody's home
Freedom will be your friend,
Not daddy, not me, just the air that we breathe
Is real

The steady hard pulse of the drums vibrated through Rick's legs and up his spine. He nodded forward and backward from the mike, until he strummed down hard on the strings in one final blast.

He turned toward the keyboard, wiggling his fingers in a three note pattern to cue the next tune, when Rick heard something snap above his head. Rick froze. He realized again, in those few seconds, that he was the spectacle, watched by a crowd. They were witnessing him being shut down. The scrim, the gray divider, was passing before his eyes. And his euphoria was diminishing just as rapidly.

"Sorry guys," the Bowery owner burst in through the side door. "But the Swedes are here. Some people walked out and we had a line demanding a refund."

Rick didn't look up from his guitar. He might smash the guy's head into a fat bloody watermelon. But he could feel the owner's gaze upon him as he spoke, "Look man, it's not personal. You were great. But, these kids are big fans of the headlining band and they thought they were stood up. If I don't put those synth twats on stage now, they'll stage a mutiny. And I'll be out money."

Automatically, Rick dismantled his guitar and motioned to the guys to do the same. He resisted the urge to tell the Bowery Hall owner, "I'll tell my father you are a fucking pig. And he'll spread the word so no one, not even the trendy idiots you book, will gig here again."

But Rick hadn't spoken to his father since he had turned eighteen. Even before then, when his mother encouraged a tangential relationship, a few weekends with dad, Rick would lock himself in the bedroom for the entire stay. Rick hated that he had no other defense, no other way to hurt this guy. They were promised six songs and they were each paid $200 up front, but no contracts were signed. The Bowery owner owed them nothing. The audience began chanting in unison for the Swedes.

Rick pushed out the side door when the Swede lead singer, his eyes lined in dark kohl, grabbed Rick's right shoulder.

"You were good," the Swede said, with a big grin.

"Thanks," Rick answered.

The Swede released Ricks' shoulder. As Rick moved past him, through the hallway, he heard it. "Really," the Swede shouted, "almost as good as your dad."

Rick welcomed the wind that whipped against his forehead as he jerked his guitar along the street to the equipment van. The kids lining up for scalped tickets didn't even blink as he walked by. His legs were pumping even stronger than when he was playing on stage. If he attempted a marathon right then, he'd win first place.

He should have decked the Swede.

DIVERSIONS

She was leaning against the bassist's blue van, one patent black pump skimming a door.

Rick could always recognize her by the tight jeans or black trousers she wore tucked into dangerous heels, paired with her slick dark hair, which stopped just under her tits. But he wouldn't have been able to pick her face from a line up, even though her breath often warmed his neck, just millimeters from his lips, in the middle of the night.

"Hey you," she said, and lifted a hand to wave.

Although he had spotted her, Rick walked directly to the back doors of the van where the drummer was already loading his set and Rick's acoustic guitar. She was the only one whom Rick told about the concert, besides Lola, because he trusted Lola more than anyone. Lola always joked, in a mock Texan drawl, "Rick, honey, I am your number one fan, baby!" And she'd slap her tush with one hand as though to say, "Giddy up!"

Rick stopped short of slamming his electric guitar on the van floor. The adrenalin pumped through his forearms and had found no release against the targets that had instigated his fervor. If he hadn't hesitated, even for a few seconds, he might have broken the equipment.

Not that it would have mattered. To most, Rick just served as a conduit to his father. The night Rick met the model at a party, he had checked the tunes she had downloaded to her computer music player, and he had discovered three of his dad's top albums in their entirety. She told Rick, of course, that she had no idea about his dad.

She sauntered around the vehicle and was standing behind him now in anticipation. He could smell the gardenia oil that she usually dabbed behind her ears and on her lower abdomen.

Rick imagined her stomach. It was flat, completely level, marked by a belly button the size of a miniature jellybean. It had been snipped perfectly eighteen years before, when she had come into this world, via a town hospital in Kansas.

Her pussy marked fresh terrain since she bled drops, equal in size to two quarters on his white sheets, the first time they had sex. She had no one else with whom to compare Rick, and that made her worth more than the average agency girls. The average agency girl valued at one night. This girl clocked three times a week, for the past month.

But Rick still wouldn't allow anyone to call her a girlfriend. Rick didn't believe in girlfriends, just temporary distractions.

"Hey," he said, grinning.

He turned around and pulled her frame down, her hips pressing against his groin, which stood three inches lower than hers when she wore heels. She had to bend her knees into the van doors to reach him. He kissed her full on the mouth.

His dick had found no relief since he had graced the stage. If the guys hadn't surrounded the van, he would have unzipped himself and pushed himself inside the girl right there.

"Hey, man where to?" the bassist shouted as he got into the driver's seat and the guys loaded up the back.

Rick took the girl's hand and walked her around to the front seat where he pulled her crescent moon rear onto his lap. Her gardenia cut the mix of smoke and interior vinyl.

The engine spit out three va-vooms, with the pump of the gas, as though it had been rotting inside an antique Chevy instead of a BMW cruiser. The bassist had spent his most recent trust fund installment on that BMW van, which Rick called "the equipment hearse."

"I can't believe they shut us down like that," the bassist muttered, " I can't believe…"

Rick put up his left hand, almost brushing the bassist's ear, to quiet him. The drummer, the second guitar, and the keyboardist sat shoulder to shoulder, like economized kids, behind Rick, the girl, and the bassist. One after the other, they pulled at lit cigarettes.

"It's bullshit," the keyboardist said. "The way we were just stopped like that so that no one even knew…"

Rick punched the armrest next to him. "Fuck it," Rick shouted. "I don't want to talk about any of this. But we're not playing any gigs at that shit hole again. Got it? I don't care if we're opening for the Stones."

The bassist pulled out, onto Houston Street. The lamps lining the wide lanes illuminated billboards of half naked teens staring down from scaffolding forty feet above the street. Tourists usually remarked upon them, while New Yorkers took them for granted, much in the same way—further uptown—Broadway lights became commonplace to residents. But that evening Rick found each giant, symmetrical body, intertwined in denim or underwear above him, to be especially mocking.

Rick swung around to the back seat again. "Not one fuckin' word more about tonight or that place. Got it?"

"Yeah," they all said in unison.

"My place," Rick instructed.

He thought about going to Roxy's loft instead, to rock out an underground show there, among their friends, to resolve the insult of Bowery Hall. But Roxy had left him a message not to contact her for two weeks.

"I'm locked down to make art," she said.

Rick chuckled as he thought about what Roxy called art. Sometimes her creations amused him since they represented Roxy's mood swings so uniquely, like tiny medicine bottles filled with individually prescribed poison. Identifying them and the moments that inspired them comforted Rick, made him feel like he had participated in particular life cycles.

At other times, however, her sculptures invaded boundaries he strived to maintain. And it was at these times, he'd disappear from her for months. This time Rick's crew couldn't blame Rick, tell him that the audience didn't appreciate his "strum hum" since they hadn't even gotten to Rick's ballads. Rick usually included two or three at the end of a hard set, often at Roxy's place. And Rick's crew was always quick to mention that once Rick lapsed into the love and death tunes, people crashed on the couch or on the floor.

Sometimes he awoke in the middle of the night, bubbles of sweat covering him. In the dream he saw himself alone on a stage in front of hundreds. He couldn't determine the location but the masses would span several football arenas, armies with hazy faces.

"I'm going to play you some songs I've written," he'd say into the mike.

"They are my own stories, not my dad's music. My name is Rick Five, not to be confused with Mick Five, the metal guitarist." Then he would play his poetry, those verses that erupted from his gut about doubt, loss, and elusive love.

"Tell me you don't want me, but just don't walk away. When the music stops, I find myself in fields of distress," he'd sing.

And he'd hear nothing, not a clap, not a hiss, not a hiccup. So he would stop strumming his guitar. Glancing out beyond his microphone, he would see that the faces staring back at him—thousands of them—were exact replicas of his father.

Rick was terrified that if he went pro, he would be compared unfavorably with his dad, or worse, panned at the outset. He feared that he would never be given a chance since his ballads—what he loved—departed so drastically from metal. So he put any professional aspirations on hold, indefinitely.

"Hey Rick, where was Loles tonight?" the drummer asked from the back seat.

The girl laid her hand against Rick's chest. He folded his hands around her waist. Rick pictured Lola always up front, her giant brown eyes smiling up at him, with that golden hair falling past her shoulders.

"Yeah, I did. I think it's the first gig she's missed," Rick said.

"Yeah…" the bassist snickered, "the gig!"

The girl whisked her tongue behind Rick's ear. Rick closed his eyes, taking in her scent. He moved her buttocks against the bulge that was fighting its way upward again, between his legs. "Hey man, just drop me off," Rick said as the bassist pulled in front of his building, the only high rise on that block of 13th Street.

"You sure?" asked the bassist. "It's not even midnight yet!"

Rick rubbed his palm into the inner left thigh of the girl's jeans. He inched his hand up toward the silk skin cushioning her spine and down to the crescent moon rear. Her dew grazed the tips of his fingers.

"Yeah man, I'm sure," Rick said as he opened the van and lifted the girl from his lap.

GENETIC TESTING

Rick walked her backwards to his king sized mattress with the overwhelming mahogany headboard that her mother had shipped him. Each time they did it this way.

He pulled off her heels, then her jeans and panties in one swoop. He whisked off his tee, unbuckled his belt, and threw his jeans to the corner of the room, which left him bare since he wore no underwear. Then he lifted off her shirt and asked her to undo her bra while he placed the pumps back on her feet.

That's when he could gaze upon her. His pulse surrendered to her milky white frame against his duvet. And the neat triangle of her bush, the only dark sign post, led to her pumps.

He strode his fingers up and down the sharp instruments of her heels, then skimmed her ankles, finally pushing them to the sides of the bed as he bounded toward her perfect bush and sucked her perfect clit with his less then perfect tongue. Flick, flick, flick. He licked her until she started to vibrate. With his left thumb he clumsily plucked at the inside of her left thigh. He formed a right fist around his shaft, pulling ferociously until he mounted her.

"Ah, ah, ah," she sucked the finger he placed between her lips. His palms grasped the juicy flesh of her rear and he rode her quick, quick, slow. Quick, quick, slow. Then quick. Rick felt as though he were swimming through an electric current that bounced him a little further toward the sky with each thrust.

"Ugh!" Rick bellowed and came. As he pulled out from inside her, thick milky semen spread across her belly, crossing her jellybean. His wiry dark curls collapsed forward to cover her button tits.

She grabbed at his hair, pulling strands as though she were

unraveling plastic coils. Rick wondered, as he always did, if she had enjoyed their sex. Half his father's chromosomes linked his genes, but he had inherited none of his more impressive masculine attributes, neither in height nor in girth. At eighteen, Rick had measured his dick, which then rested just short of four and a half inches long and considerably less thick. And it grew about a half an inch more in either direction, when aroused.

"Wow," said the girl, who now tapped his drenched neck, which made his breath quicken. A slight musk tinged her floral oil and as Rick breathed in the feral residue of her armpit, it reassured him that something did in fact transform within her, at least physically.

"Rick, you're incredible," she whispered.

Rick wanted to ask her what made him incredible, exactly. His white man's afro, his stubby frame, his library of Faulkner and Proust that he secretly hid at the back of his closet, the original Bob Dylan vinyl albums his mother had bequeathed him, the ballads he wrote that nobody wanted to hear, or the roses he nurtured at the Cape?—another passion he shared with mom.

He rolled off the girl and grabbed the pack of Marlboros from the back pocket of his jeans, still crumpled on the floor. He lit one for her first, and passed it back to where she was still reclining. He smoked his own on the edge of the mattress, with his back toward her.

Rick looked at the electric clock, which read just a few minutes past midnight. The girl was babbling something about an ad campaign, that she had arrived at the "go see" also known as the model audition, in a dress. The agency had wanted to see her in jeans so they had sent her home.

She told Rick the same tale every time he fucked her. Her ma and pa lived in trailers but still believed in the church. They thought premarital sex meant you'd burn in hell. But she had told her ma that Rick was a rock star and made beautiful music. Her ma had said, "If he's famous, it means people love him, so it's okay to give it to him."

All Rick could do was prop himself against a pillow and tuck her head into his armpit, as he strummed her shiny hair. If she clutched him tightly, he'd graze her forehead with baby pecks from his lips. But there was nothing he could say that could connect them, set them on equal ground. She had spread her legs at will, and he had taken, repeatedly.

"Let's cuddle," she whispered in his ear.

Rick wanted to call the guys. But then Rick thought about his father, how many girls dad had left in hotel beds, in closets, in vans, all of them half naked and longing. His father never specified to Rick, but his attitude supported the idea that these girls got what they deserved. They got to fuck, suck, strip, strut about for a rock star, as if five minutes of a rock star's attention, could accrue into an actual treasure, like shares of stock. As the girl's hands pressed against his middle, Rick resisted the urge to jump up, to run out the door, and down the block, naked, if necessary.

Rick kissed the girl's forehead. He couldn't just toss her out or abandon her, even if half his genes dictated that he could get away with it. Rick was not a rock star. Rick was not his dad.

MESSIAH

Lola liked the way her vein looked, seaweed green, hungry, and bulging against her ivory forearm. Unlike her more noticeable charms, the vein infused Lola with hope.

Since she was a child, people always told her she was prettier than the baby on the Gerber mashed pears bottle, the one with the apple cheeks. But for as long as she could remember Lola wanted to be free of Nabakov's curse.

"Honey, I'm going to call you Lola instead of Lisa," her mother had told her when she was nine and they were living in San Antonio Texas, where her father was stationed as an army general and her brothers attended military academy. "That's short for Lolita," Mamma had said. "The gal so alluring that even a grown man gets tricked."

"Stick it in," Lola begged him. She and the bar back had smoked hash, taken ecstasy, and snorted coke before (Lola hated the way people chattered on coke, about nothing, for hours). This was the last uncharted territory. But he had been afraid to give Lola gear.

"You're not ready yet," he had said for weeks. But since she had moved in, she could no longer stand the temptation, just under her nose.

"Stick it in!" she yelled, as she wrapped the thin white kitchen towel around her wrist a little tighter. The bar back dipped the needle into half of an empty can, which he had washed and filled with water and heroin. The owner of the bar where he worked kept a steady personal supply and in the past month, began to share with the staff.

The bar back and Lola sat on the floor of a closeted space

furnished with one mattress. Lola bit her lip. She breathed heavily through her nostrils, as though it were sea air she was inhaling rather than the vinegar tinged dampness from the floor of a bedroom in Williamsburg.

"I don't know Loles," the bar back said, as he laid the needle on the edge of the filling can. Lola grabbed for it, but he slapped her hand.

"Please, please," Lola said, and she started to whimper in a way that her mamma used to call "a false start", as a warning that if Lola didn't quit, mamma would really give her something to cry about.

With one hand still wrapped around the syringe, the bar back rubbed his free palm on Lola's shoulder. "I just don't want to hurt you, Lola. That's all."

She recognized the sorry expression on his face, like a dog who was about to piss in the house. It reminded her of her brother after he had shown her his penis and asked her to ride it like a pony when she was in grade school.

"If you don't stick that needle in my vein in the next five minutes, I will scream so loud, the cops show up," she threatened, "and I will never talk to you again."

"Just look the other way," he said. "Over your shoulder but not at me. Wrap your arm tightly, but not a strangle hold. Like this."

He pushed his fingers into the towel, right below her elbow. Lola realized that if she gazed back, he'd hesitate again, but she hated not seeing how he was manipulating the gear.

"Lola, just look out the window and count to ten, backwards," he said. He swabbed her forearm with rubbing alcohol, as she watched the groups of kids—around twenty-three, her age— strolling the gray expanse of Bedford Avenue. They seemed to stride aimlessly, the same way Lola had when she had abandoned the University of Texas her freshman year. Lola always heard that in New York, you could reinvent yourself. So she hitched all the way to Times Square. The starting ride cost as little as a laugh for a joke, and ended—six hitches later—with a blowjob for a john. But she had refused to do more than that.

Lola's voice assumed a soft lilt as she began to count: "Ten…

nine…eight…seven…six…"

On five, it pricked, and she felt it cool as he lifted the edge. "Keep counting to the window," he instructed. "It doesn't burn, does it Loles?"

"No!" she said and shook her head as she continued, "Four."

He pushed the needle in further.

She felt the drug burst through her like a meteor. It bubbled under her skin. It pumped to her heart, descending and transposing into a sweet wave. And she felt cradled within an expansive tender womb.

The sensation numbed her. The sides of her lips curled upward in a smile she could neither resist nor possess. She froze outwardly, all the while sensing a warm gooey current lathering within.

"Loles."

She heard the bar back but she didn't move.

"Loles?"

Lola perceived him not as being next to her but as an echo. The sound circled but could not contact her directly.

The beautiful demon spun within. Lola clutched her abdomen, lurching forward in an attempt to arrest the burn that churned through her intestines. Her arms and legs tingled. And, an acidic paste, like pickled tar, covered her tongue and spewed from her lips into her lap.

"Loles, this always happens the first time," she heard him say as she retched. But he sounded even farther away this time.

Lola threw her palms into her own vomit as she drooled more paste on the planks beneath her. She crawled a couple steps forward, then stopped to emit more, marking a route of speckled yellow that led her to the bathroom.

The entry to the bathroom was just a foot from where she shot up. But the line Lola crossed as she pushed her knees ahead on the floorboards felt like several stages of enduring death. She had placed herself on Christ's road to Calgary willingly.

When Lola gripped the doorknob, her temples seemed to pulse out of her brain. And, once she maneuvered it open—twisting to and fro with one sweaty palm from the unmarked arm

—she placed her head against the floor to temper the vibrations. The tiles sprouted a thin veil of mossy dust. But they cooled her enough so she could fasten her arms around the toilet seat. She supported herself between the cushion and unmopped tiles, wanting the fickle nausea that prodded every nerve to flood her organs, explode her into bits on the floor. Then, she could finally rest in peace.

The glorious thing about heroin, even then, in its worst moment, was that it didn't allow Lola to contemplate. The past, the present, the future didn't count, just the moment in which she existed. Supine and boiling upon the dirty floor, then eradicating —perhaps purifying her entire insides—into the toilet.

She was spanning the divide between heaven and hell, up then down again, up then down. She was unaware of how time passed between jolts, only that the force had surrendered her will.

The spot where the needle had pierced swelled and throbbed. A patch of blood had crusted there. And just when Lola was sure that she was finally ejaculating her innards—aorta, intestines, spleen, liver, uterus—full into the porcelain tunnel, it ceased.

She held on to the cushion for several seconds in anticipation of the next rush, which never arrived. Gradually, she became aware of the smell of her insides, skewered and steamed into a noxious vapor. The demon had calmed and was now scampering under her skin, in rolling waves.

He whispered in her ear, "Sleep my child. Sleep. I will cradle you."

Lola caressed him on the tiles. He massaged her heels, through her soles, inside and around her toes, up through her calves and thighs. He flattened her stomach with a firm rolling pin, which kneaded over her breasts. And he blossomed into furry fat poppies deep within her chest, that circulated into rays of electric violet, burgundy, and gold, shooting through the veins of her neck and behind her ears, to soothe her scalp from the inside.

"Loles, Loles? Are you okay? You've been in there for a day now."

Lola picked up the sound from outside the door, but she

didn't move.

    She didn't need anyone.

    She was in love.

GAMES

Lola awoke to beeping—32 messages—from the cell phone, which had slipped from her jacket pocket. She shivered and lifted herself up, until she stood next to the toilet. As she twisted the faucet with her right arm—now bruised black, blue, and a sickening green—her legs trembled. She laughed at her reflection in the mirror. She had survived her first smack. Her face waned, as though her features were blotted to exist just a little less. She was happy to fade away.

The only thing that still grounded her expression with the same ferocity was her tooth, the one she chipped running away from her brother at age ten after she rode him like a pony. She had crashed onto the sidewalk cement after bolting from the pup tent in the yard at the back of the house.

She couldn't have planned it any better then, since when mamma took her to the hospital, the nurses concentrated on the blood gushing from her mouth and not from her cotton underwear.

She had only just mentioned the blood flowing down there to mamma, and her mother clapped her hands and cooed, "Oh, Lola, you're a woman now!"

Her mother darted to the hospital drugstore and she brought back a pink box of powder scented feminine pads and a pair of clean underwear with butterflies sewn on the rim. She made a show of placing both on the chair next to Lola, who filled out the emergency room admission form with one hand, and held a soaked towel to her lips with the other.

"This is so exciting!" Mamma whopped all the way into the

clinic room, as the nurse stuck a needle in Lola's gum to numb it and the doctor, with a small metal prong, probed inside her mouth.

As she splashed some cold water on her face and gulped from the faucet, Lola heard a knock on the other side of the door.

"Loles!" shouted the bar back. "You finally up?"

"Yeah," she answered. Her jeans practically fell off her buttocks as she leaned on the sink. Yolky brown vomit stains covered the denim down to her ankles. "What's up?" she asked.

"Phone's been ringing off the hook." He spoke through the crack of the door as though he were afraid to disturb some private ritual she might have.

"Yeah? So?" Lola asked.

"So," he started. "Jarrett, your director called. Your cell hasn't picked up in three days since we partied and crazy Roxy's phone is off the hook. Jarrett found a backer to screen your film next week, like an underground film premiere."

The bar back leaned against the door and tried to peer inside.

"Whoa. It smells like a dead animal in here," he said. "Loles, did you hear me?"

Lola never expected the film, entitled *Le Sexe, Je Veux, Je Ne Veux Pas* or "I want, I don't want… sex" to ever debut in the States, other than bootleg copies that kids bought on internet sites. It played to cult back rooms in France, edited to electro tracks, morphing Lola into some kind of twisted Brigit Bardot.

A year earlier, Jarrett had dared Lola to take a thousand dollars a screw for five girls and five guys, then to eliminate the ones who didn't satisfy her on camera, like some kind of sexual game show. They had negotiated acts that didn't qualify as intercourse based on effort and duration per each sexual playmate. Jarrett had called it "the new entertainment frontier."

Lola knew Jarrett charged $150 for an unedited version, which included lots of his own personal orgy footage. And she never got a cut.

"Loles, I talked to Jarrett and he's serious about doing this."

Already, the flick had been featured as "un feu rouge" or a hot item in the French fashion magazines. Lola had been invited to showrooms to pick free clothing—Dior lace dresses, stiletto shoes, custom made coats—all based upon the joke they had staged and filmed in the bed of her perverted friend, Jarrett.

"That's ridiculous," Lola shouted back.

She stood on the toilet to open the window shaft. She clicked on the ceiling fan and tossed her moldy vomit crusted socks into the trash.

"Well, only if he pays me in heroin," Lola said as she undid the latch and pulled him inside.

Sex always took Lola out of her body. Even while she seemed to participate, for Lola, sex remained a spectator sport, which is why she didn't mind being paid.

But heroin required no acting. Heroin birthed Lola into existence.

"Thank you. Thank you," she shouted as she knelt down and kissed the bar back's palms.

The bar back raised an eyebrow, so Lola tempered herself.

"It's just that…" she said as she rose. "I like it. The drug's good stuff."

He continued to stand there in an uncomfortably stiff way. She kissed him behind his ear and whispered, "Baby, you made me feel good." She knew the smack had nothing to do with the bar back, thank God. Smack lived entirely independent of him or anyone else. Smack had set her free.

"Forget the drug right now Loles. You're a star." The bar back began, ignoring her affection. "This film could be big for you… for us. I could get the guys to play some music, me, my roommates. You just have to tell Jarrett."

"Damn!" Lola yelled.

She suddenly removed her hands from the bar back's grasp and gathered her mobile phone from the ground. Besides Jarrett, Rick had called several times.

"I missed the gig," Lola said. Her voice descended an octave. "I never miss the gigs."

She pulled a crushed Parliament from her back pocket and

opened the medicine cabinet to find the lighter she had placed on a shelf already crowded with razor blades, shaving cream, and loose rubber packets. She lit up with her left hand since her right arm still ached. Then she tossed the lighter into the sink.

"Whose gig?" the bar back whined. "Rick Five?"

"No!" Lola said, tapping his shoulder playfully with her free hand. "The Five Fuckers! Now let me take a shower... alone."

Throwing her cigarette butt into the sink, she pushed him even further out the door and closed herself in. In that moment, Lola realized that she missed Roxy. Roxy was the only person with whom she didn't mind sex, if you could call their kisses and fondling sex. It was more like kids going up and down a see saw. At any moment, one could propel the other higher. And then they would jump off and roll together in the grass, finding themselves wrapped in each other's arms, under a sprawling elm. But Roxy had kicked her away from the tree, even temporarily.

Nowhere was safe.

GRUB

He waited for her at the back of the greasy spoon on St. Mark's Place. He always took the last booth, with the ripped red vinyl cushions, away from the NYU students and street stand vendors with their skullcaps, pierced tongues, and all around black garb.

Lola grinned when she spotted him, at the back of the room, an obscure dot with round black shades, peering from behind a laminated yellow menu.

This place, at present time, was known informally among them as 'Rick's office'. He always chose the least trendy spot on the planet, and then lodged himself there.

She wouldn't tell him about the heroin since she knew as a kid, Rick had issues with his dad and the drug. To hide the blemishes and marks, she had worn the bar back's long sleeved thermal undershirt beneath the dark Martin Margiela blouse she had gotten free of charge from a fashion showroom.

The undershirt beneath the blouse gave Lola a husky effect, as husky as she could convey in a size two frame. Beneath the undershirt her forearms prickled. She was worried about shivering or scratching in front of Rick and giving it away.

Common substances tied her to the bar back and his apartment. But once their effects wore off, she missed the city, the real city, Manhattan. Roxy had convinced her that Brooklyn served as an abyss of wannabes, those who aspired to be noticed but blended into one another, like shades of wheat in a cereal bowl. And yet Williamsburg wheat—found at various organic diners, dive bars, and music halls that dotted the area—were distinctly styled. The girls wore vintage newsboy caps, mini skirts, and oval toed Seventies boots, which they scrunched at the knees. The guys sported ripped jeans, rock tees—preferably original tour shirts—and longish Mod rocker hair, just like the bar back.

In fact, the bar back could have been anyone. When Lola preferred anonymity, the bar back seemed preferable to Roxy, or even Rick. But Lola had been gloriously anonymous for three days and she wanted to apologize to Rick in person.

"I'm so sorry." She bent over to kiss Rick on the cheek. "You know I never miss a show..."

He shrugged and motioned for her to sit opposite him.

"It's okay." He handed her a menu. "We were shut down after one song for some girly band. The whole thing was a waste of time, so I'll let you off this time."

He stressed the word "this." She knew he had noticed her absence. Within minutes of her arrival at gigs, he'd always spot her, then personally escort her to the front row. Or he'd enlist one of the band to bring her to a coveted spot. He once told her she was his good luck charm. And in the year that she had known him through Roxy, he had never tried to sleep with her.

"Where's the twit?" Rick asked.

"He's rehearsing with his roommates. They're playing music this afternoon."

"Aaah! Music!" Rick gasped and widened his eyes.

"Look," Lola winked. "He has a right to try to sound like you!"

Rick grinned. "Getting the usual darlin' ?" he asked, referring to her regular of three eggs, bacon, sausage links, and hash browns, all fried with extra butter. It was the only thing she missed about Texas: the fat.

Lola shook her head.

That afternoon, the thought of fried everything, extra grease, made Lola want to vomit all over again. With only one kitchen fan running, the joint suffocated with that particular mixture. Even the smell alone would sicken her.

"No. I just want some dry toast, with grape jelly on the side."

Rick stared at her for a moment.

"Okay," he said.

She wondered if he was suspicious. But he launched right into conversation. "So Rox has been holed up for a week, eh?"

He took a sip of his coca cola. "Heard from her at all?"

Lola shook her head. "She's totally cut me off," she replied, as she sipped from the glass of tap water on her side of the table. She felt as though she had a hundred little bugs crawling under her skin. It was different than the times she had tweaked on meth or coke. This sensation rotated more like a spindly rash, but she didn't dare meet the challenge under her shirt. Rick placed his black frames on the table. "You know Loles, this gallery thing is serious. Her dad hooked it up, and... and..."

"And what?" Lola asked. Since she sensed he was uncomfortable with what he was about to divulge, she leaned in toward him. It proved helpful since Lola was able to knock her forearms against the table rims to directly calm the itch.

He went on. "It's not like she's showing these doll sculptures to us, to her friends."

"Yes, I know," Lola said, attempting to wriggle as imperceptibly as possible against the edge. "Didn't you burn all of her sculptures in a bonfire once at the Cape?" she asked him. "You know she never forgot that."

Rick's pancakes arrived with a side of links. He dug in with his fork. "Yeah, and I don't mind them now," he said, "because I understand how she derives them, and I need to respect her process. To her, it's art. And to me, it's her expression so I would never fault her, but I just can't... I just can't."

Lola banged her forearms on the booth a few times, so it would seem that she was only trying to be dramatic. "You just can't what, Rick?"

He speared the last link on his plate with his fork. "I just can't see," he started, "how a gallery would take those things seriously. I mean...They're creepy." Rick shook his head again. "Not to me, necessarily." He went on as he played with the fork in the link. "But to most people, don't you think?"

Lola hid her forearms under the table and scratched where she could, while trying to absorb Rick's reaction. To Lola, Roxy's dolls represented evidence that Roxy, with all her wealth and opportunity, was as broken as she was.

"I like them," she said. "I know most people would find them bizarre, but that's probably why I don't. What the hell is art anyway?"

"I guess," Rick said. He hesitated, before he continued, "I guess you're right."

He shoveled a mouthful of flapjacks into his mouth. As he spoke a little syrup dribbled to his chin, so Lola wiped it with her napkin.

"Hey, Loles," he said. "You haven't eaten your toast."

Lola shrugged, using the opportunity to rub her forearms back and forth on the table again.

"I need to go to the ladies," she said grinning.

As soon as she got through the swinging lavatory doors, Lola scrunched both sleeves to the elbows and she spotted several red bumps on both arms, which looked like an allergic reaction. She would have to stop by the drug store to buy some cortisone crème. She thought about the explanation she would give Rick for why she needed to get back to Williamsburg.

She felt herself blush as she excused herself from him.

"Rick. I've got to go," Lola announced standing before the booth. "I don't feel that well."

Rick placed his hand on Lola's punctured arm. She struggled not to squeal as his firm grasp fanned the flames of her irritated skin.

"Come back to my place. I'll take care of you." He winked. "All day cable."

Lola couldn't risk him finding out. She jutted her hip to one side, like she was about to twirl a lasso. "All day cable, huh?" She started. "It's just that rehearsal's finished and he's waiting for me, and…"

Rick shook his head. "No, no, I get it. The guy's an ass but I'm not going to interfere."

Lola knew it wasn't over, that he wanted her to change her mind, so she pulled a couple dollars from her back jeans pocket and she placed them by Rick's water glass. She knew full well this attempt was the quickest way for him to get rid of her. Rick shoved the money into her palm and kissed the back of her hand. "Get out of here!" he said. "Now, out, out!" If Lola liked guys, if she really liked guys, how they knocked each other out just for fun, how they bragged and fetched beers, the musky scent of them as they felt inside of her, busting her apart at the seams, Rick would be the one.

And since he never tried to touch her sexually, she'd always like him best.

SWAG

It had been weeks since Sarah filed the dinner party story—still a month from publication—when she got the phone call from Roxy, "Hey Sarah, Lola's getting some clothes sent over today from the fashion houses and I thought it would be fun for you to help us pick outfits for her film premiere."

Sarah also got a message from her editor, who had heard through other sources that an underground party featuring *Le Sexe, Je Veux, Je Ne Veux Pas* would take place at an undisclosed location, later that week.

Sarah wasn't exactly sure how he found out. But rumors circulated around the *Tribune* that her editor hooked into an aspiring twenty year old menswear designer who frequently crashed Roxy's parties.

Sarah's editor left word, "Sarah, I've heard your girls will be hosting a film party soon. Find out all you can and call me."

"Ah, so now they're my girls," Sarah thought as she played it again.

His voice lathered into the answering machine with a pubescent giddiness. The theme excited him, even though Sarah knew certain aspects would need to be modified for the *Tribune*, which attempted to distinguish itself as intellectually superior to the tabloid papers.

The message elaborated, "You realize that with Roxy and Lola, we are watching the birth of New York fashion icons, don't you Sarah?" It ended with, "Don't worry about the orgy theme. We can get around that somehow. Maybe quip about how Lola's filmed with her clothes off but she truly shines in Dior."

As Sarah rang Roxy's buzzer she heard the phrase over and over in her mind: "Lola's filmed with her clothes off but she truly shines in Dior." It made her feel like a man who wears excessive cologne because underneath, his unwashed armpits stink. Her editor wanted her to seduce her way into a scene that titillated him and then repeat only what he considered to be the glamorous elements.

As the elevator opened, Roxy was leaning against the dining room table, tapping the toe of one brown stiletto boot against the hardwood. A belt cinched over skintight black jeans obscured half the image of Rick's dad playing guitar across her chest.

"Hey Roxy," Sarah said.

Sarah nodded to the shelves behind Roxy, which had been covered with a long white sheet. Roxy whipped around. "That? Oh, I've been working on some new art."

"Well, I'd love to see what you've done," Sarah began. Roxy grabbed Sarah's hand abruptly.

"No!"

Sarah wanted to ask Roxy why she was being so secretive. But something in the urgency of Roxy's fingers, now entangled within her own, stopped her. They lurched toward the accordion wall.

Roxy was dragging Sarah though a forest of hung fabric. Rolling racks surrounded each side of Roxy's bed. Lola—summarily seizing dresses, skinny skirts, and tunics—ignored their arrival. She pulled one after the other from the racks as though they were paper towels instead of clothes worth thousands of dollars. A pile surrounded her of the discarded and impressive.

In her head, Sarah inventoried every conceivable type of lace, bead, brocade, and silk, ruched into curved architectural wrinkles, in pastel shades of robin's egg blue, ballet pinks, and dense creams. In her deliberate fashion, Roxy lifted a couple sleeveless dresses which looked like fancy saris and threw them behind her on a pillow, so she could prop herself higher on the mattress. The Dior labels swelled into Sarah's vision. She could hear her editor's excitable voice reminding her she was required to douse cologne on the stink, to play reporter, then air brusher.

Meanwhile, Sarah the friend just wanted to hang out and play dress-up. As much as the dolls intrigued Sarah, she viewed Roxy as a wealthy bully with control issues. And the idea of touting Roxy's celebrity for celebrity sake, or painting Lola as the ultimate fashionista by sweeping her orgies under a rug, irked her. So Sarah purposely chose a more passive route. Sarah knew that just by showing up she could dangle the carrot: the gold letter of the *Tribune* that seemed magically inscribed on her forehead. Roxy still swooned in the imagined glare. So she especially didn't want to gift Roxy with any more superfluous press.

Lola lit a Parliament while she pushed a couple of the racks back. Sarah fought the impulse to cup the ash into her own palms so the black sot would not hit the fabrics.

"I told them not to send Lola any black." Roxy said, "It washes her out and I find she fits the image of dewy ingénue best."

Roxy winked at Lola who pirouetted around. Lola, as if just noticing her, motioned her right hand sideways to Sarah, and mouthed, "Hey." As she did this, she burned a black hole in the rose chemise in front of her.

"Yeah, ingénue best," Lola said, ignoring the damage she had done. She took a drag from her cigarette. "I'm just a slag in swag," she chortled. "How much of this do you get to keep?" Sarah asked.

Sarah reached out for a dress, feeling the delicate materials and rough gemstones play against the webbing between her knuckles. Sarah noticed Roxy raise an eyebrow.

"A whole butt load," Lola announced as she threw a dress on top of her turtleneck and jeans.

"Why the hell are you putting that over your clothes?" Roxy asked. "Just take them off." But Lola ignored her and danced around the bed in a frothy pink number, the frayed edges of her denim jutting over her bare feet.

That's when Sarah noted the boxes of shoes lined below the one rack. There must have been fifty of them, the priciest names from London, Italy, and Paris. Sarah could feel the back of her neck getting warm. "How the hell did she get all this?" Sarah asked.

The words tumbled out before she could stop them. If Roxy's

stare could have cut, she would have slashed Sarah in two.

"I know. Funny isn't it?"

It was Lola who replied. Her cigarette stub, which she had tossed near some Christian Louboutin shoes, still flickered, just missing the edge of the box. "I really don't get it," she said. "I really don't. I figured you might be able to explain why there's so much interest."

Lola emphasized "interest." Roxy stood up and began nervously checking the labels of the clothes tossed on the bed. "Have you seen the film yet?" Roxy snapped at Sarah, who had remained fixed, feet planted firmly between Lola's rack and the Victorian mattress.

Sarah was overcome with a desire to evict Roxy, to throw her into the guillotine elevator so she could be alone with Lola. Lola seemed to question her own celebrity as much as Sarah had. For a singular moment, Sarah surmised that she and Lola shared a perspective, as unlikely as it might be.

Lola realized she hadn't earned it, which generated in Sarah a certain kinship. Lola possessed the same real life flesh, blood, and guts as Sarah—salt of the earth in disguise.

"Did you see the movie yet or not?" Roxy screeched.

"No, I haven't," Sarah replied, as her gaze took in a pair of peach velvet platform shoes at the foot of the bed.

Sarah had resisted downloading a version of the film on the Internet. A voice inside her head told her it would interfere with her prescribed depiction of Lola as a socialite. Sarah could only betray herself in limited ways.

"Well, the screening is here, tomorrow night at 9 pm," Roxy said. "For a select group of people. You can come, but you have to promise not to write about it."

"Why not? You invited me here today," Sarah asked. It seemed that Roxy now dangled her own golden carrot. Roxy slid off the bed and stood before Sarah. She placed a hand on her shoulder.

"Because," Roxy said, lowering her voice, "Because I invited you here as a friend, as someone who grew up down the road from my cousins in Bryn Mawr. You are a soul sister who escaped to the city like me."

Sarah wanted to laugh at Roxy's reverence of this whole scene. As much as she considered reporting on Lola's fancy wardrobe as a gross endeavor, she also didn't like to be bullied. That's when the alarm sounded.

"You're no soul sister," Sarah countered. "You're a trust fund brat from Connecticut." Lola cackled, tripping over the bottom bar of the rolling rack.

"I promise, Sarah, I'll give you other stories and access to everyone," Roxy continued without argument. "But some things, the after hours things, aren't for the press, You understand don't you? I'll make exceptions for you, just not this time as a writer."

"Just tell me this," Sarah asked. "Why did these fashion houses send all of the clothes if you're not inviting press?"

Roxy clicked her tongue, then answered, "The designers want to see Lola and our friends in the clothes, especially if they run on the party pages. I have one guy from a French photo agency who will be shooting for the fashion magazines an hour before the screening. Then, I will personally escort him out. But you... you... I consider you...one of us."

Lola stood directly behind Roxy. With her hands on her hips, Lola tossed her head from side to side, mimicking the words as Roxy spoke. Before Sarah could respond, Lola threw a couple lace frocks at Sarah's chest. "Hey Sarah, what size are you?" Lola asked. "They sent over so many, there must be something here you could fit."

"Yeah," Roxy said.

Roxy squeezed Sarah's shoulder. "Just take them," Roxy said. "No one will care. Just promise me you won't write about tomorrow night. I'll let you know what's safe to cover, okay?"

As Sarah surrendered to the peacock blue lace of the dress, the voice in her head said, "Why not?" The *Tribune* didn't allow her to take gifts from fashion houses. But she reasoned that this counted as her own experiment, that the afternoon did not correlate with official time.

Roxy, the rich girl, had been dressed down and Lola, the "it girl" seemed humble enough. So, in a sense, that day, they had become equals.

"Try them on in the bathroom," Roxy said, pointing to the doorway.

As Sarah attempted to shut the bathroom door, two clunks prevented it from closing entirely. Lola had thrown some shoes to her.

"Take these too, bitch!" Lola screamed and laughed.

For the brief time it took her to pick the shoes up from the floor, Sarah felt guilty. But as the smooth interior lining of the dress caressed her breasts and she slid into the black velvet pumps, she transformed like Cinderella.

"Besides," she told herself, "if the *Tribune* ever found out and fired me, I could sell these clothes and pay rent for a year."

But as she gazed upon her reflection in the full-length mirror on the back of Roxy's bathroom door, she knew that she'd never sell these beautiful things.

DEBUT

Sarah threw her editor off the scent. She told him that the girls had postponed the movie screening for some time in the next couple weeks, and that she would keep him posted. At first, he argued that he had heard differently, but then gave up that line of reasoning. "Well, Sarah. My source is somewhat inconsistent. And you know, I trust you."

She realized that the source in question must have been the young boy he had been trailing like a wolf. When she considered the possibility that this kid might identify her, she remembered Roxy had mentioned that the list for the screening would be tight. Extra crashers—Lower East Side kids and Williamsburg "riff raff"—would be shut out.

Sarah also decided that she would skip the movie entirely and just show up for the post party. There was only so much she could embellish. If she missed it—or say, for the benefit of her editor, she had been entirely incognizant of the film debut—he would not be able to accuse her of forgoing her press duties.

Not to mention that the thought of a sexual reality game—a try out orgy—flashed in Sarah's mind as something so starkly authentic, that no amount of Dior could paint Lola as a fantasy icon for her again.

At midnight—the witching hour for the in crowd—Sarah heard "oh, oh, oh" echo throughout the elevator shaft. Sarah sashayed from side to side uncomfortably as the stiff triangular lace of her Dior dress made its own muffled noise, like crumpling paper.

The bodyguard in the lift with her, a black guy—wide and

solid—had been manning the door with a friend who checked Sarah off the guest list. When Sarah heard the moans, she nervously shifted her eyes toward the bodyguard. He flashed her a big toothy smile. "These chicks are nuts!" He shook his head back and forth. "But I work all of their parties, for Roxy, in case shit goes down ya know?"

Sarah nodded, wondering what the neighbors were thinking, with sex aching through their radiators. And then she remembered that Roxy's father owned the building. Roxy had plenty of leeway.

Sarah walked into the apartment, which was filled with fifty or so guests. The place was pitch black in spots, except for the votive candles that lined the walls and a massive screen that flickered just above the carving table.

"Oh, oh, oh," Lola gasped on film. Her eyes glazed over and she pouted, while some scrawny guy with pasty skin rode her doggy style on a wide bed. He pinched her nipples with his spindly fingers.

"How's that for you, baby? Do you feel my cock, baby?" he asked. It was too late for Sarah, who had witnessed the evidence. She had nowhere to run.

Throughout the apartment, women styled in Bond-like slinky dresses and heels huddled together with guys wearing ripped denim and fancy sneakers. They discoursed and clinked glasses —as though a rock video was playing—instead of Lola on a twelve foot screen getting screwed up the ass.

Sarah requested champagne once she made her way to the bar set with vodka, beer, and two bartenders. Their stolid expressions betrayed any awareness of the full-length erotic acts played out just a foot away from them. Somehow, this struck Sarah as more eerie than the guests ignoring it themselves. But Roxy had explained to Sarah the previous day, that no matter how the film played out, she required—specifically in the invitation—that everyone keep their clothes on and their composures contained. Jarrett K, the director, had filmed a social experiment. And in that sense, it should be considered and viewed as art.

Sarah crept toward the sofas, circled the windows, and then

moved past the accordion wall, where she spotted Lola—perched on the bed like a 1920's debutante—in a pink tea dress. She blew smoke from her Parliament cigarette to the ceiling. Despite the grunts and moans on the other side of the wall, Lola seemed disconnected entirely. At Lola's feet, Sarah recognized the bar back from the shoot. He sat, like a dog attending.

On the other side of Lola, on the bed, Roxy was bent over, her red hair jutting forward as she inhaled some white powder. She threw her head back, snorting, and wiped each nostril with the back of her hand, Beside her, Rick turned around. He had been leaning against the wall behind the bed. Sarah hadn't noticed him initially.

"What the fuck is press doing here?" he bellowed.

He was gazing directly at Roxy, as if not acknowledging Sarah would make her disappear somehow. Roxy shook her head and tried to hand him the bill in her hand, which she had been using for the coke. He motioned her away. With a sneer, he turned toward Sarah. It made her feel especially misplaced. In that moment, she wished that she had arrived earlier and had taken notes for her editor. She wished she still had a purpose, a real reason to be there other than the opportunity to debut two Dior dresses, one of which she was wearing, and a pair of $500 shoes.

"No, it's cool Rick. Sarah's cool," Roxy said. "She's not working tonight. Right Sarah? Sarah, do you want some coke?"

Sarah felt Rick's gaze critically take in her every gesture and the alarm sounded again. This time, the voice in her head questioned, "Who is he? Some slacker with a rock star dad."

As story research, she had downloaded a few songs from the internet that Rick had recorded with his band. The lyrics, desperate stabs at self discovery, could have been easily mounted the decade before the electronic boon, as the flip side of his high school locker door.

"So Rick," Sarah asked. "Do you ever record your own music or do you just cover your dad's songs?" He didn't answer but she won the point. He averted his eyes, and Sarah's fingers, which had been clenched into fists at her sides, released.

Sarah tried to meet Lola's gaze but, sitting on the bed, milky eyed, she had disappeared. Every rise and fall of her cigarette appeared catatonic. The Lola who had giddily sampled the outfits with Sarah the previous afternoon, the girl who mocked herself and played with her bounty like a child in a candy store, had left the room. In her place was this shell of a female in a silk dress.

Roxy now outreached her arms, which held long lines of cocaine on a flat ceramic ashtray in one, and the rolled bill in the other. "Sarah, you want some coke?" she repeated.

Rick watched, Sarah implicitly understood that if she took just one line, he'd release her from his attention again, since then he'd have something on her. So she grabbed the tray and snorted half a line, which tickled and stung her left nostril. She brushed the other half away with the pinkie shielding her nose.

"Hmm," Rick grunted and sauntered around the accordion wall, past Sarah, to the main room.

"Uh, hi Lola," Sarah attempted to greet her, as she handed the tray back to Roxy. Roxy shoved it under her bed, then hooked Sarah arm in arm. "Don't worry about her," Roxy said. "She gets like this sometimes. Come into the living room with me."

The coke frisson racing through Sarah's temples perked her up a bit. But she generally tried to avoid the drug since the next day it dropped an ax through her head, like a hangover but a hundred times more potent. She had inhaled one little bump, only as a rite of initiation, to prove that she had arrived, not on duty, but for social means.

She snaked through the crowd with Roxy, who now pulled Sarah close to her side and chatted a mile a minute. She introduced Sarah as her new best friend. While such saccharin pronouncements from anyone else would have struck Sarah as juvenile and somewhat offensive, from Roxy, it seemed charming, as though she were honoring Sarah at the ball.

Sarah saw designers she had covered in the pages of the *Tribune* and a few indie actors. Roxy introduced her to Jarrett K., the director, who chuckled when he met her.

"I'm telling you," he said as he pushed his fingers through his shag hair. "Sexual reality is the wave of the future. You can print that in the *Tribune*."

"She's not working tonight Jarrett!" Roxy said as she punched him in the arm.

Sarah tried to prevent her eyes from seeking the screen, especially since the film was in its third repeat of the evening. An Asian woman was now kissing Lola, and Sarah found their light panting easier to ignore than the skinny guy's cock rant.

Rick was sitting on a couch and on his lap reclined a brunette. She wore six-inch crocodile pumps. To Sarah, she didn't look much older than sixteen. The girl roped her never ending legs over Rick's slight frame but still seemed unsure of her power. As Rick rubbed one of her calves absentmindedly, Sarah caught his glare.

"He hates me," Sarah said to herself.

Why should she respect him just for having a famous father? As they moved beyond the head of Roxy's carving table, Sarah gleamed another set of eyes, like two turquoise bulbs, illuminated by the screen. Darkness had cast a shadow around much of the rest of him.

"Don't go near him Sarah," Roxy said and pulled Sarah up to the bar.

"Why not?" Sarah asked.

She focused on her champagne glass, rather than directly into Roxy's face. Sarah didn't want Roxy to identify the click, the irreversible click that happened when someone attractive noticed her in that way. Sarah had already decided, for that evening that she would allow herself to play as they played.

"He's a scum bag," Roxy said. "And I have no idea how he got in here." Sarah was tempted to ask, "How about that porn scum Jarrett K?" but she did not want to create a scene. "Who is he?" she said.

"The guy's called Darius Lamb. He's a fashion photographer from Beverly Hills. But he's been banned everywhere because he objectifies the models in the most disgusting way. No one likes him. So, don't go near him."

As Sarah and Roxy faced the direction of the screen again,

Darius smiled at Sarah. It was one of those cat ate the canary grins, or as Sarah would term it, "I know you've clicked into me too" signals. As much as Sarah attempted to maintain a serious face, her lips puckered upward. Lola had just gifted a blow-job to the male front runner "king cock" on the big screen. And, turquoise Darius, raising an eyebrow at Sarah, bit his lip.

"That's it. He's out of here!" Roxy yelled and threw her champagne glass to the floor, which exploded into shards around her ankle boots. She grabbed Sarah's hand, leading her toward the lift, and pressed a button.

"Yeah," said the voice on the wall speaker.

"I need you to get someone out of here," Roxy said.

An instant later, the guillotine opened and Sarah's lift companion, the big safe guy who told her "these chicks are nuts" strode into the room. Roxy pointed at Darius, who, unaffected by the pantomime obviously directed toward him, didn't flinch.

On screen, Lola was languidly sucking a blonde woman's breast, as though she had just stumbled upon it while sleepwalking. The bodyguard hoisted Darius off the chair by the forearm and dragged him to the elevator. Darius screamed to Roxy, "Hey Roxy, where are your freaky voodoo dolls, huh?"

Then he caught Sarah's gaze again, as his tall limbs stumbled behind the bouncer. He never averted his attention from her, finally blowing her a kiss, just before the blades closed out his visage.

"Oh, oh, oh," Lola gasped on screen.

"Thank god!" Roxy said, and threw her arms into the air.

Sarah waited a few minutes, until Roxy excused herself to the bathroom. And then, Sarah made her exit.

DIASPORA

"Hey."

The voice startled Sarah as she walked out of Roxy's building past the two bouncers. He had been leaning against the brick wall of the dry cleaner at the corner. Again, his eyes struck first.

He threw a cigarette to the ground, which he extinguished with one of his sneakers. His scuffed tennis shoes stood out like odd Western cousins on gray urban cement.

"I was wondering how long it would take you to get out of Roxy's peep show," he said.

Sarah laughed out loud and then stopped herself since she didn't even know him. He pushed away from the wall and moved toward her, sticking out one hand to shake hers, which were still buried in her coat pockets.

"Hi, I'm Darius."

Sarah nodded. "I know."

It slipped out before she wanted it too. Immediately, he raised his eyebrow and grinned at her in that devouring way.

"I'm Sarah."

She put out a hand, which he bent over and kissed. This made her giggle. Ordinarily, she never giggled.

"You're Sarah Rosen, the one from the paper, right?"

He raised an eyebrow again as he lifted his mouth from her fingers, still securing her grasp in his.

"C'mon, let's get out of here!"

He gestured to a cab and Sarah held on to him. She knew she should probably free herself and run away. That way, she would retain her mystery. But something direct and confrontational in his manner, the same quality that seemed to irk Roxy, propelled her to him.

"Roxy's a freak ya know," he said when they got into the cab. "But you, you're absolutely beautiful."

"Thank you," Sarah said, appreciating the Dior, which brought her to life.

"Miss Rosen, are you Jewish?" Darius asked. The Miss Rosen *schtick* made her want to laugh again. She hesitated initially, however, as she took in his olive skin and full lips. She wasn't compelled to be cagey with him, as she was most of the time with everyone else. This time, she didn't even attempt to determine a motive.

"Yes," she said.

"I'm Jewish too you know." He gave her hand a shake the way a father might lift a tot's arm to emphasize something especially intriguing.

"Where are we going?" Sarah asked as the cab sped through the streets to the entrance of the FDR Drive, the eastward highway, heading uptown.

"The Carlyle Hotel." He winked. "We can sit around Bemmelman's Bar, and gaze at the animal murals."

"The animal murals?"

"Don't you appreciate art?"

"Well, sure but…"

"After all, we're all animals." He smirked. "Stinking ridiculous animals."

"No argument," Sarah replied.

They arrived within minutes. Releasing her hand, Darius circled to the other side of the taxi at 76th street to lead Sarah out in front of the hotel. The porters—men who had worked there long enough that their hair had whitened with the rusting of the gold leaf—bowed together in uniform. Darius, winking at Sarah, bowed back at them.

She found herself giggling again. She couldn't help herself. She was already drunk from the attention, especially because everyone thought him inappropriate. The whole world, even the domain of beautiful people, proved inappropriate to Sarah. But Darius opened himself up, warts and all.

Darius' sneakers, those foreign bodies like Tupperware, encased his feet and seemed to plaster themselves into the crimson carpet. As they sunk into two fat gold armchairs, Sarah expected a porter to tap Darius on the shoulder, to say, "Sir, we observe a strict dress policy here. You'll need to leave."

But since no one came—even after he had ordered two kir royals, delivered without hesitation, "Here you go sir. Very good sir," to their seats, and even as he inquired to the waiter. "Which Beluga caviar tastes fresh tonight? Not so fishy?"—Sarah kept peering around, waiting for the inevitable. Then where would they go?

He stretched back on the cushion. Sarah wanted to pull Darius forward, to tell him he shouldn't get too comfortable. But he pushed himself far back and with one hand, shoveled a mound of caviar between his lips. Sarah took in his every swaggering motion. She surmised that he had the confidence of wealth behind him. He could have been shoveling fries into his mouth at a fast food joint.

"Sarah, tell me everything about you... Don't you write for the *Tribune*?"

"Yes," she said.

"Sarah, they don't appreciate me over there."

"Why not?"

She held her breath, wondering if he had drummed up all this fanfare to grill her about work.

"Because I shot some things, exaggerated too much. Home layouts with teenage girls baking pies. I asked them to pour honey over their fingers, lick them. I just can't get excited..."

Sarah listened and pushed herself to the edge of her seat. He scooped more caviar into his mouth, a fat spoonful, like pudding. Sarah wondered how he might kiss, with those lips, which were perfectly full and aligned. With her own spoon, Sarah nipped at the specks of Beluga, which had escaped to the edge of the bowl.

"What do you mean you can't get excited?" she asked.

"Perfection doesn't interest me," Darius said.

who town · 103

"You're a hypocrite," Sarah said. "You're a fashion photographer, so perfection does interest you."

He grinned and tapped his utensil on the side of the table. "I've sold my soul."

"So you admit you're a hypocrite?" she asked.

"Yep."

Sarah drew her fingers over the lace trim of her dress. She had made her own Faustian deal and she was wearing it.

"I'd rather be following the army, African tribes, people who earn enough sweat to fill buckets," he offered. "But I ended up in fashion. So I do what I can. When they don't allow me realism, I embellish beyond what is required. I ask girls to suck honey thumbs. Or guys to stick plastic cocks upright in their pants."

"You mean dildos?" Sarah asked.

Darius laughed. "Yeah. Can you think of a better way to show a hard on?"

He licked three specks of fish egg that dotted the right side of his mouth. He nodded his head toward her, as if he wanted to stress the force of his creative experiment.

"Yes, okay Darius," Sarah said. "But just don't call it art."

"Yeah." He snorted loudly. "Jarrett K seems to have that covered. I can't compete with that!"

He was ripping back the curtain right before her eyes. She wished she had the guts to do the same. She wanted to stop lying. If she could become more like Darius, she'd have the guts to rebel, to tell the story she surmised and not the one dictated by her editor or the mass hunger for blind unquestioning celebrity. She had flashbacks of Lola's naked calisthenics and repetitive moans, which after an hour sounded as provocative as computerized music piped into suburban mall speakers. Still, he had the net of a Beverly Hills trust fund to pay bills. He could afford to risk it.

"Ah Sarah," he shook his head at her. "But you don't care as much as the rest of them."

"Care about what exactly?"

"Getting laid."

"How would you know what I care about?" Sarah pushed her

hips to the side of her seat so she now sat diagonally rather than practically knee to knee with him.

"Because I've noticed," he started. "When that sculptor chick struts before anything famous, you just assess. Hands off. Like you've drawn an imaginary line around yourself that says, not one step closer... and that's... and that's..." He stammered. The hesitation made Sarah feel as though she elicited a particular power over him. "That's...that's..."

"What Darius, what?" she asked.

"That's ...special."

Sarah didn't want him to realize he had affected her. But she informed him without a syllable. Her face and neck flushed. He watched her, never averting her gaze, until his beautiful lips curled up just slightly in a satisfied smile.

"Would you stay with me in my suite, for the weekend?" he asked.

Standing behind her, like a guide, as though he had blindfolded her, he walked her towards the king sized bed, which was covered in a thick burgundy velvet duvét. He crossed his arms around her waist and pulled her against him. They fell onto the mattress, two clothed bodies lying sideways, clinging together.

"You look like my mother," Darius said, as he unlocked his grasp for a moment to untie his white shoes. He flung them at the wooden pawed feet of the Louis XIV chairs. Sarah reached down and dropped her pumps. "What's that supposed to mean?" she asked. "That you're attracted to your mother?"

Darius laughed and threw back the covers. He grabbed for her again and pulled her beneath the sheets.

"My mother was the most beautiful woman in the world," he said. "Until I met you. You are my Jewish princess. And princesses should be respected. You're not like the rest of those fashion tramps."

Sarah froze, even as he kissed her neck. If he hadn't tempted her ideologically and if she could resist him physically, she might have questioned his distinctions and bolted out the door. But she had entered Darius' cocoon, another dimension. It felt comfortable.

who town · 105

She could smell the mint on his breath from the candy they had shared in the elevator. As he pressed against her in the bed, she detected his hardness arching upwards at the base of her spine.

Roxy would never speak to her again.

"Nobody needs to know about tonight," Sarah told herself.

He pulled her closer to him and she closed her eyes.

"You're more honest," Sarah told him.

"More honest than what?" he asked.

"Than me," Sarah whispered. She hesitated, "Sometimes I'm like a zombie. I see what's going on around me and all I'm ever asked to do is construct images. It's all such bullshit. I'm waiting for them to wake up, to wake up and get…"

It was as though he had read her mind. "Get the joke?"

Sarah smiled so widely that her cheeks hurt.

"Yeah, I know," he said. "You want to know why I waited for you outside the party?" he asked. "I never wait for anyone."

Sarah wriggled silently. He squeezed her, halting her movement. "I'm sick of models who want the easy road to fame, between their legs. You don't need me."

They cocooned for two days under the covers, ordering room service, watching movies, and kissing in pajamas. Darius had purchased them from the hotel. And yet not once did he even try to feel her up. She heard him masturbating in the shower in the morning, and if she wasn't so terrified of losing herself to him, she would have walked in and put his hand on her instead. Maybe that's what he wanted her to do. But she was too afraid. On Sunday morning, still ensconced in bed, he pulled her face so close to his that his pupils became two hypnotic mounds of crushed blue stones. "Sarah, should we just leave? Get out?"

"What do you mean?"

Darius released her and sat up on the bed. "I mean, let's go away. I'll buy us both open-ended tickets. You could take a leave from the paper and I can float us for a couple months financially. Then we can find our own stories. You can write and I'll take the photos. Forget the embellishment. Real life. Truth."

Darius jumped up and paced by the side of the bed, briskly

crossing back and forth in front of the French chairs.

"Sarah, just think how great it would be to explore India, Africa, parts untouched."

She figured he couldn't be serious. But her stomach tumbled and twisted with the thought of it. She had regimented herself, buried her emotions, to become somebody, to escape. But then the media machine had taken her hostage. She didn't want to churn out more. And neither did he. Darius plopped himself on the mattress and grabbed her hand. "Sarah, I'll get the tickets in two weeks when I'm back from my shoot in St. Bart's and we can leave next month. What do you say?"

"Really?" she asked.

"Yes!" he shouted. His lips swallowed hers like soft warm gel.

"Okay." She said, still woozy from his kiss. That afternoon, Darius loaded a knapsack with her Carlyle pajamas into the trunk of the town car he had summoned to drop her off, so he could pack before flying to his Caribbean shoot.

He took a little bit of her breath with him when he kissed her goodbye.

"I'll call you when I'm back in a couple weeks!" he said, winking. "And I'll buy our plane tickets!"

Sarah waved out the back window of the car like an overeager child. She wanted to believe him. If she stayed with the *Tribune*, her mind might shrivel. She didn't care anymore.

When Sarah returned to her barely lit studio in the West Village, with new eyes, she examined the small white stove in the corner, the pull out sofa with the paisley pillows, and the rolling rack of clothes in front of a fireplace that did not ignite. Collecting celebrity fireflies barely paid the bills.

She smoothed out the straight A-line skirt over her cheap sofa cushions before picking up the telephone to call her editor. Above the non-working fireplace, the clock marked five p.m. He had left a message that morning.

"Hello," she said. "It's Sarah."

She heard the editor clear his throat, the same sound he made before rejecting one of her story ideas.

"Yes?" she asked.

"Sarah, I'm afraid I have some bad news."

She halted her automatic reflex to speak again. She knew he was about to torch her. She thought as long as her fingers summoned her attention to the expensive lace covering her body, she would not collapse. "Sarah." He cleared his throat a second time. "Sarah, I'm going to have to let you go. I'm going to have to cut your contract."

She said nothing—she did not have the breath or the voice to ask why. She just picked at the frock, which for one night had transformed her into Cinderella.

"I know about the film party Sarah, and I know you were there," he said.

"You deliberately lied to me."

"Not deliberately," Sarah replied. She thought about how she never wanted to witness Lola grinding naked with several people in a bed, that it could never fully marry the iconic images he had prescribed. And that experiencing it would compel Sarah to write a human story, not a fashionable one.

"I had no intention of seeing the film, none," Sarah said as she pushed herself to the edge of the couch. "I just got a message from Roxy to stop by to hang out. Not as press."

"Sarah, as long as you work for me, you are always press."

"I can make it up to you," she pleaded.

Sarah wanted to salvage what she could. Even if Darius' adventure fantasy came true, she did not want to be terminated, just like that, not after struggling so long to make it this far.

"Well, how do you propose to make this up to me, hmm?" The editor asked. Sarah could envision him, rolling a clove cigarette as he concocted some lively Moulin Rouge moment with Lola, Roxy, a clothing designer, and a whip. "Will you promise me that you will cover the next underground event they host, no matter what, and I mean cover it damn well? Hmm?"

Silence.

"Sarah, I need you to chronicle the je ne sais quoi fabulousness of Roxy and Lola. Is that clear?"

Sarah wanted to tell him she had taken two fancy dresses and two pairs of shoes and that she too had been an "it girl" for the night. She wanted to tell him that she passed in the same fashion as Lola and Roxy, that the dress made the woman. It was not the woman who made the dress. She wanted to say that disco had died a long time ago. And it was time he stopped lusting after youth and young boys. She wanted to tell him what she had told Darius: "This is bullshit."

Instead, she said, "Yes. I understand."

Sarah's editor cleared his throat one final time.

"I'm glad it's clear, Sarah. You are on probation."

CAMP

Lola snuck out the night of the screening party, back to the bar back's Williamsburg hovel. She had only returned to Roxy's for a week. The two weeks apart hadn't made Lola any more desirous of Roxy's comforts.

She would eat half a dish of Captain Crunch cereal in the afternoons and not a bite more. She refused expensive Japanese dinners and gazed at the television for hours.

Roxy knew that Lola, the bar back, and his friends did plenty of coke and whatever else was dumped on them after hours. But their binges usually aroused a need in Lola to cling to Roxy that much more. After a couple days away, she'd return supplicant and grateful for every cup of miso soup, the vitamin packs Roxy would administer, or the masseuse Roxy would hire by the hour.

Roxy knew this time was different. Upon return, Lola had slept for two days straight, with heavy sweaters pulled over her white cotton nightgown, shivering at intervals. But with her gallery interview looming the Monday after the film screening, Roxy decided not to trek to Williamsburg like a mother hunting for her lost young. She would have requested that Lola leave the loft anyway, for the afternoon, when the gallery owner and his curator arrived to assess her work.

The doctor had told her that this opportunity marked a chance to assert her independence, not just from Lola but also from her father. The pressure made her want to pull the knife on herself again, but she resisted, telling herself that she couldn't risk strange scars on her body. Even if she wore long sleeves and covered her throat, she'd be aware that they lurked underneath.

Right before the party Roxy had hidden the new pieces in her collection—twelve in all, her own tribe—under the bed. She had stored them in a box that her great grandmother once used as a luxury cruise trunk. She had wrapped each sculpture carefully in wads of tissue paper and placed layers of silk between them.

And now, as she unraveled them, ready to display them on the shelves behind her carving table, Roxy's fingers trembled. The doctor had told her she should give herself over to whatever emotion erupted, especially with the figures that depicted her father. But as Roxy examined the first few pieces, she felt an overwhelming desire to rename them, to disguise herself, to reinvent her history.

Roxy jumped when the doorbell rang. She had arranged the statues on the shelves in the order she had constructed them, beginning with the ones representing her father, and ending with her mother.

She had vacillated between two outfits: a moss green wrap dress and heels, which her mother had allowed her to wear to the country club over the Christmas holiday or skinny black jeans which gathered at the ankles, over her boots, and Rick's lucky concert tee. She decided on the latter since it fit the public image she had constructed. The green dress fit Rose, but the gritty gear fit Roxy.

Roxy hit the door buzzer. As she placed her palms together, she detected the perspiration between them. Quickly she rubbed the sweat on her jeans. She told herself if they hated the work, she would trek up and down the West Twenties through Chelsea, on her own, until a gallery signed her.

She held this thought as she stood before the lift, watching it open. But a fear still rose within that prompted her to throw the work out the window, to plead ignorance to the merits of her efforts, and to tell her visitors she had nothing to show.

The gallery owner, in his late Fifties, dyed his thinning hair black. The sun of the loft shone on his widow's peak and added ten years to his appearance. Roxy smiled widely, fakely. She pushed out her right arm.

"Hello, hello. Welcome!" she said. It sounded disturbingly like her mother when she hosted bridge nights.

"Well hello Rose. Your father has told me good things."

Roxy knew that her father had never glimpsed one of her sculptures. Short of the crayon drawings she used to give him when she was a child, he had never actually seen it. His appreciation of her art existed as a concept.

The gallery owner motioned to his curator, an Asian American woman, whom Roxy guessed had just peaked at forty. She had bangs, long ironed hair, and straight solemn lips. The curator nodded, and Roxy did the same, saying again, "Hello, hello! Welcome!"

"So," said the curator in a muffled voice. "We would like to see your sculpture."

"Of course," Roxy answered, wondering at the curator's laconic tone. Had her own enthusiastic greeting startled her into some kind of altered passivity? The gallery owner however, immediately picked up the slack.

"Yes, yes, Rose. Do show us!"

Roxy led them to the shelves. She mentally inventoried the work before she dared to describe them audibly. The first three—called 'Slob' 'Prince Charming' and 'Adulterer'—represented alter egos of dad.

'Slob' resembled W.C. Fields, with a bulbous reddened nose and a drunken charlatan's smile. Roxy had carved in nicks of drool painted yellow, which dripped onto his black jacket and trousers, for an especially ghoulish effect.

The flip side of 'Slob' was 'Prince Charming'. 'Prince Charming' possessed smooth features, painted sky blue eyes, a straight carved nose, and a line for a mouth, which perked slightly upwards for a charmed effect.

Roxy sewed together a navy linen suit cut stiffly on the body, since 'Prince Charming' was impenetrable. No woman could resist him. And since he kept his emotions in check, he always remained in control. When 'Prince Charming' turned horny, he became 'Adulterer'. Adulterer's perpetual hard on stuck straight up, like a miniature pencil, the kind used for standardized tests. His penis parted the white terry robe Roxy had sewn for him. He clasped a wooden cigar between two fingers of his right hand, which was elevated almost to his mouth, just a millimeter hole for smoking.

Roxy attempted some sculptures of Lola, which resulted in two figures, both sporting strawberry blonde braids and white cotton aprons. She thought about carving the crooked tooth into both of them, but decided to save that intimacy for herself. Instead she cut a closed smile on one of them and carved hands holding a slightly protruding belly, which Lola did not have. Roxy called this one 'Full'. The other braided figure frowned into a deep sharp curve and her palms faced upwards as if questioning the clouds. Roxy called her 'Wanting'.

Four pieces—which Roxy had placed together in a group—represented 'Wannabes'. They remained androgynous, in denim jeans, tee shirts, painted eyes but no mouths whatsoever and hair below the ear line that could have fit either sex.

Following 'Wannabes' came 'Idiot One'. He represented the bar back, a stick figure who wore a diaper and a red tee shirt, on which Roxy had scripted the phrase "Rock On!" with a skinny black felt pen. He held a tiny carved wooden beer in one hand, which he tilted to pour on his own diaper, clipped with a large sized safety pin.

Then, Roxy crafted 'Balladeer', which Rick had inspired, a short statue with a large round head. 'Balladeer' held an acoustic guitar and his mouth formed into an oblong opening. She had felt good the day she created 'Balladeer' which soon reversed itself, since the last statue Roxy carved sported hollows instead of eyes. Just sockets marked the center of the face, which was partially shrouded by a bobbed canary blonde wig. Roxy's mother had inspired it. And Roxy had named it 'Ignorant'.

"We're ready Rose," said the gallery owner. Roxy nervously rocked back and forth on her heels. She felt like a student called to answer questions on a chalk board before a classroom.

"I'll start with the first three," she said. I can explain them if you'd like." The curator picked each one up for a few moments, fingering the fabric and running her hands over the wood. She turned 'Wanting' and 'Full' upside down and Roxy needed to resist the urge to grab them from her grasp and to reposition them upright.

"Hmm," The gallery owner repeated over and over.

"Let's examine some of these more closely," he suggested.

The curator raised 'Slob' into the air. "So, Rose," she said. "Tell me about this sculpture. It's quite depressing. What inspired it?"

Roxy thought about the weekend nights when her father came home in Palm Beach, how he stumbled and drooled, his eyes wild, his shirts undone. Although her mother told them all to go back to sleep when he erupted into the house like a bull on full charge, toppling vases and sometimes falling on stairs, Roxy wished he had never come home.

"Um, well, it's a parody of W.C. Fields," Roxy said.

As much as the doctor told her this experiment connected her to her father emotionally, for good or bad, Roxy could not betray him, especially since he had set up the meeting.

"Why W.C. Fields?" the curator asked. "Isn't he a little before your time?" The gallery owner chuckled and wiped his brow with the back of his hand.

"Well," Roxy said. "W.C. Fields is an honest drunk. And today, they are a dying breed. So I wanted to show him as a fool but also a tortured fool."

"I see," said the curator and picked up 'Adulterer'. "How about this one?" she asked. "I suppose you are going to tell me that this one is Hugh Hefner."

Roxy crossed her arms and dug her nails into her forearms until they stung. Her nails were too short to scratch her way out of this, but digging them in as far as possible was the only way to prevent her from crying on the spot.

Roxy scrambled to the other side of the curator and cradled 'Wanting' in her hands.

"You see this one?" Roxy asked. "She represents the need we all have, the empty parts. Her sad expression shows she's given up but her palms are still raised to the sky, expecting."

Roxy then picked up 'Full'. And she's the twin soul of the other girl, she's what happens when that expectation has been met."

"And this guy," Roxy lifted 'Idiot One', "This guy represents the boy who has been stunted."

Roxy pulled at the safety pin. "You see, he's the spoiled child inside every man."

The curator raised an eyebrow, then pursed her lips in a controlled smile. "I see."

"Never mind that," the gallery owner intervened. "Rose, we have a group show coming up in a week. And it just so happens that there's part of a wall free in the back room."

"Actually, it's a very small space," the curator interjected. "But I suppose we could make room for a few of these."

Roxy summoned up enough courage to ask, "Are you sure?"

She felt as though she had been holding her breath the entire time. Like steam, her energy was dissipating. Best to lose it all now if the curator changed her mind, best not to exhibit at all than to suffer anxiety publicly, on the curator's terms.

"Well Rose," she said. "They do have a certain camp quality to them."

Roxy exhaled deeply and allowed herself to smile. If the curator had formed an opinion of them, even to use the word "camp", then they must have triggered something.

BOUNDARIES

By mid afternoon, two days after her gallery audition, Roxy grew tired of pacing her floor and meeting what she considered secondary friends for drinks.

Her pride, which had whittled away much in the same way she had whittled away at wooden blocks, could only hold her back several hours before begging Lola for attention. She had telephoned her father's car service to deposit her in Williamsburg. She asked the driver to drop her at the corner, so she'd seem less conspicuous as she walked half a block to the bar back's building.

"I'll call you when we're ready for a pick up," she told the driver.

Although Lola had run back to Brooklyn quicker than usual, Roxy comforted herself with the idea that Lola had felt cast away. And the remedy involved some demonstration on Roxy's part.

She rang the bell and the bar back answered "Yeah" automatically buzzing her through without inquiry.

The overflowing garbage cans in the vestibule stunk of sweet rotting bananas and sour milk. She teetered upon each step in her spindly boots on her climb to the third floor. When she spotted a mouse scurrying along the second floor hallway, she almost tumbled backwards.

All the buildings here resembled one another—brown stucco monoliths occupied with dreamers, most of whom Roxy felt would waste away anonymously.

The bar back's glazed pupils identified Roxy from behind a

chain lock still fastened on the door.

"Oh, it's you," he said. Roxy wasn't sure if he had been expecting a drug delivery or someone he owed money since he looked especially startled. Just when she assumed her appearance had eased his mind, he slammed the door on her face.

Roxy kicked and slammed her fist.

"What the hell! Let me in! I need to see Lola."

"Yeah, uh, hold on a sec."

Roxy could hear his footsteps trampling throughout the space. Bags crumpled as though he were gathering several at once from the floor.

"I know you're a pig!" Roxy shouted and kicked the door again. "You don't need to tidy up for me. I don't give…"

And just then he opened up.

He clasped two full plastic trash bags, which ran from his hips to his ankles. The perspiration from his arms, locked within a heavy wool sweater, made him stink like three-day-old socks.

Roxy edged him. "Where is she?" she demanded.

"She's sleeping."

"Where?" Roxy asked as her eyes flashed around the musty living room, a ripped couch to one wall, newspaper and sheet music strewn on the floor. She noticed drops the color of ink lining the hardwood to the bathroom, where the trail had stopped.

Roxy turned the knob of the bedroom door. As she peered at the whited socked feet turned out like a ballerina in first position on the mattress, Roxy forgot her anger.

"Hey you," Lola said in a groggy voice.

She gave Roxy a lopsided smile. Roxy jumped up on the mattress and squeezed Lola by the arms. Lola wore a similar turtleneck to the bar back. She squirmed in Roxy's embrace.

"What's wrong?" Roxy asked.

Lola had pushed herself upright.

"Nothing, I'm just tired."

"Tired in general?" Roxy lowered her voice. "Or tired of me?"

"No it's not like that," Lola said.

She gazed back into Roxy's eyes and her expression, newly dulled in just a few days apart, cast a shadow between the two of them now.

"I just need some time," Lola said. She started to massage her elbows. "I just need my own space sometimes. It's all gotten way out of hand."

"What's gotten out of hand?" Roxy asked.

"The party, me, what?" Lola nodded, still rubbing her arms and blinking vacantly. "The party was hard…" Her voice trailed off.

Roxy wanted to leap up and net her like a butterfly. Now, Lola was rebelling? She was rebelling at the moment Roxy needed her most.

"You could have told me and I wouldn't have hosted. I wouldn't have allowed Jarrett…"

Lola placed a hand around Roxy's wrist to stop her in mid-sentence. For almost a year, Roxy had ignored her art to minister to Lola's needs, to keep her afloat. After all Roxy had accomplished to promote Lola, just a two week break, and Lola didn't believe Roxy held her best interests. Roxy felt that Lola was punishing her unjustly.

"What about him?" Roxy asked and nodded toward the bar back in the living room.

"He's easy," Lola answered. She smiled absently.

"I got a gallery show," Roxy announced in a chipper tone. "Next week." Roxy hoped she could prompt Lola back to their natural comedic rants. She wanted Lola to inquire about the quirks of the sculptures.

Lola nodded and grinned. "That's great," she said, but she still seemed far away. "I'll be there, Rox."

Roxy realized that she would not be able to take Lola home with her that day. She was already drifting back to sleep. "Okay Loles."

In that moment, Roxy understood that she no longer possessed any power over her. She decided she would not pressure Lola until after the opening, or she might lose her completely.

She gingerly brushed her lips against Lola's forehead. "You know where to find me when you wake up."

OPENING

The curator picked four of Roxy's statues: 'Wanting', 'Full', 'Idiot One', and 'Adulterer' for the show, which was entitled "Subconscious Travels."

The name "Rose Sullivan" with the phrase *emerging artist* in italics had been added last minute to a program of four other artists, including an African muralist, a portraitist photographer, and a couple who created light installations.

They were emerged artists, most at least ten years older than Roxy, and they fetched anywhere from $5000 to $30,000 a piece. Roxy's contributions—her debut into the art world—were priced by the gallery owner at $500 each.

Roxy had joked to Rick, "I'm bargain basement. So maybe these collectors will buy a tribal mural and tack me on for a few more dollars."

But Roxy had serious doubts. She didn't dare point out to the gallery owner or the curator—whose direct tone cracked like an ice cube on the phone—that she would like to be mentioned as Roxy Sullivan, not as Rose. Her father was the only one she still allowed to call her Rose. Anticipating the possibility of seeing her father that night, Roxy had shoved a couple Xanax in her bag before leaving the loft. Her father's pending appearance, of course, depended entirely upon his state of consciousness.

"I'll try to make it Rosie," he had told her. Still, she knew better. Usually, he gave her everything but himself.

At her last session, Roxy had also invited her doctor. In

case she suffered a break down, she reasoned, she wanted him to be there. She had briefed him that her father would only be represented by one statue. And when she wailed in his office, afraid that he would think she had not succeeded in her therapy, he had offered her a sedative.

The doctor told her she had progressed, that the creation of any work meant growth. But she had cancelled her appointments for the weeks before so he would not suspect her scars. And she lied to him when he asked if she had cut herself beforehand.

"I resisted. I went straight to the wood," she told him.

Professionally, expressionlessly, he had simply pushed his glasses to the tip of his Play dough nose and softly cleared his throat.

The gallery, located on the far west end of twenty second Street, right before the West Side Highway, was considered a collector's destination. The exhibit space was intimidating in the stark way so many galleries in that area had fashioned themselves. They resembled mammoth store fronts with spurts of decisive limited color, often in the form of less than a dozen works hanging. Square lights fit cozily into the corners of ceilings that stood twelve feet high, and the outer walls were whitewashed like typewriter correction fluid, so as not to interfere with the art.

While no noise code had been set in any of them, the Park Avenue dames and critics who frequented Roxy's gallery, rarely spoke louder than a whisper. With discerning looks upon their faces, they sipped cheap wine from plastic cups. The younger and curious smoked out front. And fancy bank managers, who seemed to linger longer than others inside, picked special pieces to enliven offices tinged with olive plaster.

Roxy tried to imagine the reaction of a CEO sitting at the head of a boardroom with 'Adulterer' or 'Idiot One' on a shelf behind him as he went over quarterly reports. The image made her shudder. In a sense, she felt they'd be justified in such settings since most heads of industry cheated on their wives, like her father had done, continuously. And Roxy would wager more than half of these executives had sired idiots for sons. "Never trust men," Roxy repeated to herself, watching each guest. She prayed that Lola would arrive first.

Groups of fashion kids who worked at magazines with one word titles like 'Thrash' or 'Blue' or 'Outre' approached the entrance. They donned gold lame' bags and moon boots. They seemed to resurrect glam in the crowd of dark tailored jackets, worn by folks who had probably witnessed glam the first time around.

As more and more of these kids dropped in, appearing especially haughty, but obviously clueless, Roxy saw the curator's jaw stiffen. Roxy retreated to the back room and stood by her shelves.

With one hand she pulled the black knit dress with a bottom —shaped like an inverted tulip—far below her knees. As she clutched her tiny fist around a cup of Pinot Grigio, kids whom Roxy recognized but could not name, approached and kissed her on both cheeks.

"This work is fabulous, absolutely fabulous Roxy."

And then some said, "We didn't know you were Rose."

Roxy could tell that the ones who mentioned Rose were the ones who didn't like her, the ones she had turned away at her parties.

Roxy saw the doctor shuffle in with his wife, a squatty woman in a polyester gray pantsuit. The wife wore apricot lipstick. The vision of them together, this lackluster little couple, made Roxy doubt he could ever understand how she needed to be acknowledged in a big way.

Roxy's eyes darted around the room. The art patrons ignored her. More than ever, she desired Lola, her apparition of light.

She hugged her doctor hello and grinned at the wife too. She could not afford to lose him since he knew too much. But as Roxy heard him tell his wife, "Yes, Roxy really invested a lot of creative energy into these." Roxy hated him. He had minimized her entire contribution to psycho-babble busy work. She wanted to lift 'Idiot One' and pummel him.

She wandered away, but only a few feet, unable to stop tracking the glazed expressions as the sophisticated set passed her statues, without a blink, or worse. A woman whom Roxy recognized as a benefactor to the Guggenheim Museum grabbed her male companion's arm. Her mouth hung agape before 'Idiot One' and 'Adulterer'.

"Is this some kind of a joke?" she chirped.

Her escort grunted in the way old men often do, "Must be, must be."

Roxy thought she might crumble if she stayed by her shelves, so she forced herself to push toward the front room. She felt ashamed to be exhibited next to life infused wall murals of warriors in the bush or shadows of boxers who moved like ethereal prophets.

Marching toward the door, she paused when she overheard the gallery owner say "Rose Sullivan" from the small office to the left of the entrance.

Roxy lodged herself in the crack between this workspace and the spot where people were arriving and heard the curator answer whatever query had been put forth.

"I can't believe we've even allowed this junk to take any millimeter of space in here," she snipped. "Lower East Side garages show this kind of kiddie crap. I thought you had more integrity than that."

"Look, we got the lease on the new space," the gallery owner answered. "Sometimes you need to compromise. Her old man made it pretty clear that this was the only way he'd cut the deal."

Roxy would have been justified carving herself to bits. The doctor had been fooling her all these years, taking her money, when she didn't deserve to exist.

Rick was right to toss her pieces into a bonfire when they had drunk a bottle of whiskey at the Cape. She laughed then, saying it would free her. But it had filled her with self doubt. It was the closest Rick came to telling her she sucked. Then Roxy remembered Sarah.

"I'd love to see your process," Sarah said. No way could Roxy face Sarah at the gallery that night. She realized she probably only had a few minutes left to slip out unnoticed.

Her cell phone beeped. Rick had left word that he was on his way but that he could not find Lola. As she retrieved her messages, her hand trembled. She spotted her father walk in and she cowered further into the office crack.

On other occasions, just the sight of him boosted her spirits. It was as if he were Santa Claus and she still believed in him, even when her two older sisters didn't. Every appearance marked Roxy like a special gift.

But when he strode past her hiding spot toward the back room, Roxy sprinted out the entrance. The cold wind whipped against her as she deftly navigated between bodies to cross the street.

Even in such frigid weather, she walked several avenues before hailing a taxi. She needed to sober up emotionally. No matter how much her father sinned over the years, Roxy usually begged to have time with him. But not like this.

RENDEZVOUS

Certain things Rick would never mention to the guys: that he had paid seventy thousand dollars for a collection of first edition Shakespeare plays, that he had planted the roses in his mother's flower boxes, and that his favorite Sunday pastime was to meet his mother for tea at the Carlyle, at least once a month.

As he spotted her in the hotel dining room, an earnest smile illuminated her face.

His mother's eyes always ignited for him, which spurred a sense of pride within him. She preserved tea as their ritual. And, that Sunday after Lola's film debut, Rick had been particularly anxious to break free. The model had attempted to fry eggs and had splattered the gas range and the walls. The guys wanted to gig at his place, then watch football on his flat screen wall television.

"I've gotta go under today," Rick said. "I've got to be alone, write some music."

None of it held his interest. He and the girl had already fucked several times. After each time, she asked him if he would rather be with Lola since Lola apparently knew what to do.

"Lola knows how to get everyone off," she said.

"Christ, I don't even see her that way!" Rick bellowed, perhaps a little too loudly. Of course he had seen her that way. He repressed it. Lola gazed upon him with such grateful eyes; Rick would never want to disappoint her in bed.

"Don't say Christ," the model answered. She curled herself into a ball and pouted. "You're talking about Jesus."

Rick wanted desperately to run away. That he hadn't cut the model loose yet was an oddity. Her naiveté both thrilled and frustrated him. And just when he wanted to tell her that he was a freaky loner, that he could not commit, and wouldn't it be great for her to explore life on her own, he grew furious at the idea of her sharing her body with other men.

Just a little while longer, he told himself. And so he remained, stuck there.

"Hi honey," his mother said, getting up from the golden cushion of her chair even though he motioned that she should stay seated.

The temperature dipped well below freezing outside, and his nose had turned pink. But the floor to ceiling windows of the hotel bathed the dining room in warm light. The marble floors gleamed like flattened peppermint candy.

Rick's mom kissed his cheek and she squeezed both his hands the way she always did.

"I came in to meet the girls yesterday. We went to the Moma for a Jeff Koons exhibit," she chatted, and sat down again. "Then we had a lovely dinner, this little Thai place on Sixty Third. Organic Thai, if you'd believe that." She had already ordered a basket of mixed scones and jams for both of them. A waiter in a white jacket arrived to offer Rick coffee, English tea, or green tea, which his mother had chosen.

"The renovation's almost complete," his mother said. She smoothed her hand over the linen tablecloth. "So I'd like you to take a look, Rick."

He nodded, as he pulled apart a cranberry scone, using his hands like paws, the way a bear would rip at food. She knew he hated going to the Manhattan space. The penthouse apartment represented the only thing of value his mother had inherited from the divorce settlement. Now that Rick's father had moved to Los Angeles, she had finally summoned the courage to change the design from how it appeared the day Rick had saved her from the stove.

And while his mother spent most of her time at the Cape—in the house bequeathed by Rick's grandfather, his namesake—she visited the city every two weeks in the fall and winter months.

"It's very cozy Rick. I've ordered Balinese bookshelves," she said. "And I've filled it with lilies and ivy. Not at all like before. Since you didn't want any of your father's art deco, I had a dealer sell it second hand, and…"

Rick cut her off. "What do you mean you had a dealer sell it second hand? You couldn't at least make more money from his name? That's all he's good for, his name."

Rick's mother shook her head.

"I've let go of that a long time ago. It means nothing to me," she said. Rick lodged his knife in the butter dish in anticipation of his second scone, and he restrained the urge to reprimand her. He knew she lived frugally now, despite her wealth in real estate. Rick would have gladly sold the furniture himself, hawked it at as some kind of celebrity collectible. Rick thought about how his grandfather must be rolling in his grave, that his mother had shortchanged herself again.

Rick's grandfather had taught literature at Harvard and had held a grudge against Rick's mom for attending college at the more liberal Brown.

"Both Brown and this rock boy," Rick's grandfather used to say, "are not entirely adequate."

"Rick, I want to talk to you about the memoir," she said. "The publisher telephoned the other day. Seems there is renewed interest since your father is contemplating a new tour."

Rick stabbed the butter cup with his knife so hard that it struck vertically and remained. He knew she had refrained from pursuing the book for his benefit, since before his mother married his dad, she had garnered a reputation as a rock groupie.

And in the year of her breakdown, after Rick's father screwed at Stonehenge then OD'd on heroin, his mother relinquished her polished appearance. Rick had found Polaroids—from bedroom drawers she had overthrown—photos of her with several men and women, naked. Since his father appeared in none, Rick assumed his father had snapped them. Rick ripped up whatever he found and did not investigate, but he never forgot about them. And he never discussed it with her. Maybe she wondered how those photos left on carpets had mysteriously disappeared. Perhaps she knew he had destroyed them. It was one of those things he swore he would never tell her. That and the shameful fact that when his father had lapsed into a temporary coma after OD'ing on heroin, Rick had prayed his father would die.

His mother lifted his knife from the butter dish and leaned in closer. Rick ripped apart another scone, which he had no intention of eating.

"Honey, listen. You know I was not an angel, even with your father."

"Yeah, okay," he mumbled. "But you don't have to write about it."

It was the second time she intimated a lack of innocence. The first time, five years ago—when the publisher had signed her and kept her on retainer, just in case—Rick walked out of her house. He left his guitar in the sitting room at the Cape and drove straight back to the city.

"Mom, you can have half my trust fund."

He would happily sacrifice half of the thirty thousand he got each month to prevent the world from seeing his mother in a way unacceptable to him. But she shook her head.

"Honey. That's yours. I don't want that. But I do want you to consider that I might write this book."

With all the literature he treasured, the idea of his mother penning trash would destroy him. He knocked the creamer off the linen covered table and it crashed into several pieces on the marble floor.

"No!" he shouted.

As two waiters, dressed to the neck in stiff white shirts and black jackets knelt at his feet to sweep up the china, his mother stopped him from fleeing. She grabbed both his hands and squeezed them reassuringly between her palms.

"Okay, okay. I won't do it. If you're that upset, I promise I won't."

His mother released him then and sat back in her chair to take a sip of tea, as though no disagreement had transpired.

"How's the music, Rick? Have you written anything new?"

Except for the lost year, Rick had always marveled at her composure. For a while, he thought it might be the weed she still smoked on occasion, although she never shared it with him.

"I've got a few I'd play for you," Rick said. "But I want to wait until we're back at the Cape."

He still refused to play any music in the penthouse. Rick couldn't shake the feeling that the penthouse represented the place where his father had stained her, which is what once led her to stray sexually. Now that his father led a separate life, she had become pure again.

"You write beautiful lyrics, Rick. Really something."

Rick laughed, since his mother loved the ballads, the "strum hum." He reasoned she would like anything he did. But he also knew she would prefer for him to get an Ivy League degree in keeping with her family's tradition. But he hated the idea of crowds contained in classrooms, the obedience of it. He'd rather be self taught, locked in his room with his books and sheet music, himself and the task at hand. Maybe that was the bit he had inherited from his father.

"I know you've bypassed college by so you can write and play," his mother said. "But people need to hear you besides the boys."

Rick began to shuffle his feet under the table. He remembered his reoccurring nightmare, the silent crowd staring blankly at him, each one resembling his father.

He leaned back further in his chair. Rick's mother pushed her teacup in his direction and clasped her hands in front of her.

"What about Roxy?" she asked. "She's been following you around for years. And now, when I'm in the city, I see her photo in all the fashion magazines. I bet Roxy could help you. Get you some publicity."

"It's all bull," Rick said.

Her mouth twisted in frustration. She smoothed out the tablecloth. "Look mom," Rick grabbed both her hands to stop her fidgeting, "I don't care. I really don't. I'd rather be anonymous."

Just then, a swath of electric blue caught Rick's attention.

Sarah, in a party dress from two nights ago, appeared in the lobby. Rick's mom turned to follow his gaze.

"Rick, are you interested in that girl?"

He didn't trust Sarah, but he was curious. Why was she still wearing the same clothes from the film party? He remembered seeing her leave well before he had parted at dawn on Saturday morning. And then he saw Darius Lamb step off the elevator with Sarah's coat.

"Is that her boyfriend?" Rick's mother asked.

"No," Rick said. "Just some dick. C'mon, let's go see your apartment. And no, I am not interested."

He felt badly that he had said "dick" in front of his mother since she never mouthed a foul word. He reasoned, his father had done much worse.

POSSESSED

"What do you mean you didn't know she was shooting up? How did you not know she was fucking shooting up? You live with her!" Rick shouted.

"Not really, not any more." Roxy said. Roxy twitched in a way that Rick had never witnessed before. She usually darted around, casting a measured energy of movement, even when she hadn't altered her position much. But now, Roxy visibly shook. Something else had taken over, which is why, when Roxy snatched a switchblade from her oak chest, Rick grabbed it. "This is not about you!"

Rick yelled and flipped the blade closed. He angrily tucked it in his jacket. Rick's keyboardist had stopped at a party in Brooklyn the previous evening, the night of Roxy's art opening. On his way to hang his coat, he had found Lola and the bar back on the floor of a walk in closet. They had stashed themselves under a rack. Lola, lay totally stoned, with her bruised open arm facing him and a used syringe upon her thigh.

"She didn't know who I was man. She's not right," the keyboardist kept saying, which made Roxy shake more. Rick couldn't process what was happening to Lola and Roxy at the same time.

"Stop it!" Stop it!" he yelled and shook her by the shoulders. As she fell against him, Rick detected the musk oil she used as pomade for her hair. Lola, who always looked like an angel to him, emitted smoke from every pore when she hugged him. And Roxy, who whipped everyone into submission, smelled like an orchid scented lullaby.

Rick cradled Roxy back and forth in his arms. It reminded him of his mother in the early days. He did this for several minutes, while Roxy sobbed into his chest.

"It's all my fault," She yelled, pelting him with her tiny fists. "It's all my fault! Lola never shot up before I asked her to leave. I should have never asked her to leave. I'm killing her!"

She pushed him away from her and whipped back to her chest of drawers, throwing knives on the table and nicking her right forearm. As she gripped the area she had sliced, it spurted a gash of blood.

"Oh Christ!" the keyboardist yelled.

"Clear the fucking knives man!" Rick said. Roxy fell on the floor at Rick's feet, dripping on his Chuck Taylors.

Once the keyboardist had loaded all the knives into a garbage bag. Rick started for the kitchen. He grabbed a glass from the cabinet, filled it with cold water, and then dumped it over Roxy's head. He didn't know how else to calm her down. The water at least, stopped her from sobbing.

Rick recalled that Roxy had told him she used to cut herself as a kid. But he had felt sure that the practice had ceased with therapy. Wet on the floor, Roxy whimpered at his feet.

"We need to get you to a hospital." Rick said and reached for her. But she wouldn't take his hands. She just shook her head from side to side. And she spoke in a whisper.

"No, Rick. Really. Just get the peroxide and bandages in the bathroom, under the sink."

Rick motioned to the keyboardist who returned not just with peroxide and bandages, but several tubes of various salves, including balm used to ease cow udders and sore muscles, and anti fungal yeast cream.

The keyboardist plopped the solvents and himself on the floor beside Roxy. As Rick poured the peroxide on Roxy 's wound, she breathed deeply. It was the calmest version of her that Rick had ever witnessed. In her newly sedative state, Roxy lifted a thick beige bandage with her free hand and told him to wrap the cut, then secure it with a metal clip.

"Really, Rick," she said calmly. "This happened after I had asked her to stay with that idiot in Brooklyn."

Though Roxy's eyes pleaded with him, though Rick tried to act sympathetically, with each word she uttered, internally he condemned her.

He wanted to tell her she had acted selfishly, but then he remembered the times he shut off the phone when he wanted to write ballads or poetry and the weeks when he'd disappear to the Cape. But this was different. This was Lola.

An overwhelming sense of guilt crept upon him. It was as though Roxy had read his mind when she told him, "Rick, she wouldn't have stayed with you. She kept running back to that idiot."

The keyboardist squeezed the tube of muscle balm and rubbed some on his hand absentmindedly. "We should kill that fucker," he said. "We should get the van right now and find him in Williamsburg."

"Yeah?" Rick said, raising an eyebrow. "Why didn't you take him out last night?"

The keyboardist shrugged. "He was passed out cold, and I didn't know what to do. I just kept trying to talk to Loles. She just smiled and smiled. Said something about some tent, that she wouldn't have to play in the tent anymore."

"Rick," Roxy whispered. "We need to save her."

Rick remembered how his mother had tried again and again to save his father. And how she had always failed. Junkies don't want to be saved. Junkies want to be left alone.

"I can talk to my doctor," Roxy said. "We can stage an intervention. And I'll pay for the rehab, all of it. And I'll call Sarah…"

"What do you mean, you'll call Sarah?" Rick snapped. "Why would you call that reporter chick. Are you fucking nuts?"

"No, no! You don't understand." Roxy raised her voice. It sounded strange and distorted. Rick wondered how much blood she had lost. How much blood could someone as small as Roxy lose? Perhaps she was delirious.

"If Lola knows that Sarah has witnessed the intervention, it will act as added insurance that Lola will stay clean after recovery.

Lola will know that the press has been informed."

"You just don't get it, do you?" Rick said, stepping away from her. "If it gets into the papers that she's a junkie, they'll say she's some washed up porn star and isn't it typical that she's hooked on smack."

"No Rick. It only adds to the cache."

She struggled to stand, leaning with the hand of her uninjured arm on the table, to support herself. "Sarah's a fashion journalist and in fashion, all drugs, including heroin, are chic. It can only help. It's like insurance," she continued. "Look at Hendrix, Jim Morrison, Janis Joplin, Kurt Cobain, so many of the big models."

"Yeah," Rick chortled. "They're all dead, with the exception of the models. And the only reason they're still here, is because they are barely out of their teens, and they bottomed early."

"Well, your dad's still around," Roxy said. He couldn't believe what Roxy had become. He always knew she felt the world revolved around her. At most times, it had amused him. But now she had gone too far. She was willing to sell Lola off just to benefit her image. Anxious to shut her up, to cut off her line of reasoning, Rick slammed his fist on the table.

"We'll pick her up and take her to my mother's place in Massachusetts," he said. "But you need to let me handle everything."

Now Rick felt he needed to save Lola from Roxy. He banged his fist on the table again.

"I'll handle everything," he yelled. "Got it?"

Roxy nodded feebly. She swooned as though she were about to topple onto the table. Rick grabbed her by the shoulders to steady her. He was bound to the same role he had assumed at ten years old. He had to put out a fire. He was on call again.

WILTING

Rick had to know. He needed to find Lola for himself, to witness a desperation he refused to believe.

The keyboardist had said that Lola seemed pretty banged up. The idea of her any less than vibrant made him want to crack the bar back's skull. So after leaving Roxy, Rick borrowed the band van to drive to Williamsburg. The bassist and the keyboardist begged to help him, but Rick insisted on solitude. As he went over possible scenes in his head, Rick almost crashed into two cars on the bridge.

Like his mother, Lola remained a symbol of re-flowered innocence. No matter how badly his father had behaved, Rick's mother resurrected. And in Lola's case, no matter how many people had tasted her physically, she never fluctuated for him.

Even images of Lola in Jarrett's orgy films didn't turn Rick on. It was as if the Lola on screen were a separate entity entirely, an imaginary creature. Rick thought about the afternoons when Lola would paint her toes on his beanbag chair with cherry red polish she had bought at the drug store for fifty cents. He would play guitar on the couch, and when he paused to watch her, she'd concentrate on her toes as though she were adding some detail to a masterpiece. Any small token he would give her—a chocolate chip cookie, a soda, a scarf to tie her hair—would bring her delight.

He wondered how far she had come from San Antonio. In the years he had known her, she never visited home. He sensed Texas spelled taboo. Even Roxy didn't know about her childhood. When he delicately inquired, Lola would tell him few details.

"My family is a bunch of military hacks," she said once. "They're big on family values. And mamma makes the lightest angel food cake in the army wives club."

But when he asked about her brothers, she'd change the subject. She'd flick on the television, or throw herself at his feet, rolling toward him with her blonde hair falling forward. Then she'd beg Rick to make up a song for her on the spot.

Flattered by the attention, he'd compose hokey country numbers, dedicated to her, his Texas Rose.

> *I love you Lola, Oh yes I do,*
> *But you've got bar twit,*
> *So now I'm blue.*
> *But I know deep down*
> *You're really gay,*
> *So I just tell myself no sex's okay.*

They would both fall over clutching their bellies on Rick's shag rug. It took every nerve in Rick not to touch her. But when she looked up at him with so much appreciation, he'd feel proud he had resisted.

When he got to the bar back's door, Rick rang the buzzer several times, but no one answered. He thought about waiting on the steps of the building, or spying in the van, like a stake out, until they came home. But then the idea that Lola could be passed out under a clothing rack, possibly suffocating in a dark wardrobe closet, overtook him. So he drove to the locale of the previous evening's party. This time, when no one responded, he followed a delivery guy inside.

The steps to the fifth floor loft seemed like the steepest he had ever climbed. Part of him wanted to turn around and drive away, rather than possibly gaze upon her distorted.

Rick could hear faint music, some electronic trance beat, which repeated over and over again, from the inside. Still trying to catch his breath, he banged on the door.

"Open the fuck up!" he shouted. "It's Rick Five for Lola. Open

who town · 144

the fuck up!"

There was no answer. Rick knocked again.

"Open the fuck up or I call the cops!" he shouted.

The seconds felt like hours.

Finally a thick waisted bald guy in a tank with a gold hoop earring flung the door open. Without looking at Rick he walked back to the leather coach where he had been playing a video game. Aside from the couch there were three chairs, a coffee table, and a television. The windows, which practically filled the length of each wall, had been opened to the fullest extent so the place cast a draft from every corner.

Behind the seating area around the sofa, people slumped against the back walls. Six in all lay huddled under blankets, some of them shivering, some of them sweating, all of them bleary eyed, most of them high, two of them, asleep.

Rick hovered by the bald guy, whom he had never seen before. He seemed to be in charge.

"Where's Lola?" Rick asked.

The bald guy shrugged. "Think she's back there." He pointed to the walk in closet next to the bedroom.

Rick went over and slid the door aside. At first he could see only clothes, but then he distinguished her red toenails jutting out from beneath some hanging trousers. Supine, she had been lying with her head directly under a bottom rack.

The unconscious bar back lay to the right of her, although their bodies did not touch. Rick wanted to wake him then beat him back into unconsciousness. But his priority was to rescue Lola. He placed his palms around her arches and began to rub the bottom of her feet.

"Loles, hey Loles," he whispered as he tugged her calves to pull her out. The must of the closet suspended the entire space in manly heavy wool. Lola didn't rouse initially when he softly laid hands on her. But then her open eyes—like miniature lighthouses—signaled him.

Kneeling over her, Rick lifted the clouds of greenish black, which had taken shape inside her forearms, to his lips. Gently he kissed the inside of her elbows. The dress she had worn, a frilly ivory number, had been stained with dirt and graffiti threads of dried blood.

"No pony, no pony," she said, when he picked her up in his arms and carried her out of the apartment.

The bald guy never quit his video game. And since no one noticed, Rick didn't care that he was sobbing.

CURSED

"Stick it in…" The words barely cracked through Lola's parched lips as the nurse checked the methadone drip, then placed a cool compress upon her forehead to meet the beads of bubbling sweat.

Lola had been saved, placed in Balance Hill, a rehabilitation facility started by a bunch of old hippies who had settled in Rhode Island. Some former LSD types who ran the place had attended Brown with Rick's mother. The non-medical staff were called "balancers." The balancers never spoke louder than a whisper.

Lola had been placed in a twin bed, in sparse room with no television. Next to her, another junkie was slumbering on a mattress and frame of identical proportions. Lola looked just past the anonymous roommate, out the window. The place mimicked an Ivy League University.

The balancers had strapped Lola to a chair and wheeled her around the ample grounds upon arrival. She had noticed the red brick buildings covered with ivy, all of it so easy on the eyes that it could have been cut from a postcard.

As they pushed her chair up a pathway to an entrance, Lola's bones shuddered. She felt as if an imaginary fire dragon searching for a fix had stopped spewing hot venom into her veins and that they had turned to ice. Not even the lighted fireplace in the front lobby could help her.

Deep worn sofas, that seemed to require aged Scotch served in goblets, surrounded a round chestnut coffee table with detailed brochures. The brochures listed activities, including the following: yoga, reiki, massage, oil painting, literature discussion, metaphysical healing, yogic channeling, spiritual chanting, and tarot reading. As a nurse handed Lola one from the coffee table, she overheard a lanky kid in a baseball hat.

"Yeah, the tables are round so the patients won't try to stab themselves on the edges of furniture."

Ordinarily, Lola might have cackled or answered the kid out of the blue. But her nerves tingled in every direction, like jellyfish. Moreover, she didn't belong there. It wasn't Texas. And it wasn't hell. So it wasn't familiar.

Lola looked at her night table. It had been covered with "safe items" from people who were not yet "safe to see" she had been told, until she didn't want to shoot smack again. She had received three bottles of red nail polish from Rick, a meditation recovery manual from Rick's mother, and one of Roxy's sculptures, a braided blonde with her forearms flung to the air that made Lola want to shoot up again every time she glimpsed it.

Why had they stopped her? Why had they forced her back to life? Lola could have gone on like that indefinitely, lulled into her purple haze. She could dip into the nothingness independently of men, or Roxy. And now she felt profoundly uncomfortable. Everything under her skin revolted at once.

Lola gazed down at her shaking hands, which slowly eased as the methadone warmed her. Inch by inch, it crept into her veins. But, it wasn't enough. She wanted more.

As she pushed the call button beside her bed, the girl lying just a few feet from her, by the window, spoke to her for the first time, "It's no use, you know. Don't even try it. They listen cause they know you want more drip. For minutes after you've pressed the knob, an audio device clicks in and they wait to hear you wail. They'll only come if you make something up, like you're hungry. And if you fake it enough, then they won't come at all."

The girl couldn't have been much older than eighteen. She resembled one of Roxy's preppy relatives, with her upturned elfin nose and golden hair trimmed evenly in angles.

"Just wait until you get the shits," the girl said. "It happens around the third day."

She talked a lot for a junkie. Lola overheard she had been in isolation, detoxing next to an empty bed until Lola had arrived. Lola smiled back, the best she could with her lips cinched, as sweat beaded her forehead in want.

Lola had already sized up her roommate to be one of those rich New England gals who showed up at rehab twice a year, while Lola should have been left to rot. On her own, Lola could never afford a place like this. But the curse still cushioned her, this time through Rick's trust fund. Lola gazed at Roxy's pathetic night stand beggar again. She thought about smashing it with her fist, but her arms weighed heavily and empty all at once.

When mamma had her baptized in a white cotton dress in the river, the year after she chipped her tooth, mamma had told her, "You'll always be a Lola with those desiring eyes." Lola felt she'd eventually pay for attracting those kinds of sins. And now she was paying because they wouldn't let her go on her terms.

The worms in Lola's stomach were wringing around each other. She hurled forward a little in the stiff bed until she felt the methadone kick in again, jolting her back against the two pillows that cushioned her from a stern wooden headboard. As steam seemed to peel from her forehead, Lola relented to a steady breath.

The girl across the way took Lola's momentary relief as a signal to speak. "Hey. Aren't you that French film star from all the fashion magazines?"

Lola thought to crawl under the bed, or at least hit the panic button. But then she surmised that if she just nodded and gestured, the roommate might think she didn't speak English. So Lola nodded. She smiled, mouth closed, again.

"My boyfriend jerks off to your photo," said the girl.

The girl's eyes searched Lola's face for some reaction. Lola knew it was the curse again. She furrowed her brows and stuck out her bottom lip in a way she hoped indicated that she hadn't understood.

The girl started lifting her free arm, the one not hooked to a drip. She began pulling her fist up and down and simulated panting.

"He does this!" she said. "For you!" With her index finger, as though she had cued an orchestra, she pointed to Lola.

Lola didn't dare move, not a limb, not even a quiver. It seemed like the whole world wanted to masturbate to her. And all she desired was to escape, to hide, and to eventually quit. But the more she went inside of herself, the more people dragged her out for use. She didn't know how to turn them away. She didn't know how to stop bringing them either. Seduction was the only talent she possessed. While Lola had been ashamed to use it, especially after her brother had taken advantage, after it remained the only thing in which she excelled.

The girl on the bed had finally ceased her theatrical panting and now appearing bored, turned her head to the back window.

A new nurse stuck her head through the crack in the door. A shift must have changed. Already, almost twenty minutes had passed since Lola had pressed the button. Lola's limbs, newly infused with the drip, melded into the mattress, tempting her to slumber.

"Lola, welcome to Balance Hill. I'm the night nurse," she said softly, then gave Lola her best Zen grin. "You'll see, the first couple days are a little uncomfortable, but we will rehabilitate you, promise."

The nurse lowered the room lights and bowed out the door. As Lola closed her lids, she thought "How exactly do you rehabilitate a whore?"

FREE LOVE ANONYMOUS

Everyone at Balance Hill spoke hardly above a whisper. So when the morning nurse bellowed from the hall, "Look honey. Back off. Lola's not seeing anyone for a few weeks." Lola knew that Roxy had tried to break through.

From her stupor, tossing and turning on the thick hard mattress, Lola tried to comprehend if Roxy had actually stood outside her door. Minutes later, when the nurse brought a mug of green tea and a wheat grass shot, she told Lola that her friend had been telephoning.

"Roxy sends peace."

It sounded like a Christmas card and not like Roxy at all. The nurse's wispy speech had returned. Balance Hill even went as far to say in the brochure that "voices should mimic the temperate influence of wind chimes."

The old Lola would have chuckled and pawned some nugget from the nurse about the detail of Roxy's calls. In her mind, Lola could imagine Roxy telling the nurse to shove her yogic maneuver on a shelf. The old Lola might have superficially collaborated with the nurse and empathized with her disapproval of Roxy's rudeness.

Once Roxy's attention had confirmed in Lola some sense of human shelter. But now, it impressed her as a trap. So as the nurse relayed the message, Lola just smiled and took a sip of her green tea. It tasted like herbal scented rainwater. She would have preferred a syrupy Coca Cola and a couple of cigarettes.

Lola wasn't sure what she missed more: smack or her

Parliaments. When she glanced at the brochure in her wheelchair the night before, her eyes moved over the curriculum to the smoking room on the site map. Once they pulled the intravenous drip, she'd head there first.

Lola placed her fat round mug on the saucer with a deliberate gesture, and she pushed the brownish green wheat grass shot to the corner of her tray, to indicate she wanted none of it. She only desired to roll over to sleep some more. But the nurse intruded by sitting on the edge of the bed. A balancer brought another tray to Lola's roommate that not only featured tea and wheat grass but a grainy milky oatmeal concoction that Lola had renamed "outmeal." With the exception of an added line on her pinned tag that spelled NURSE the nurse wore regular clothes. The doctors donned white lab coats, but they all fostered the idea that staff should not be held on pedestals.

To Lola, the nurse looked forty-ish. She wore faded cornflower blue jeans and was small and quick. She would have called to mind one of those yappy dogs except that her voice had certain restrictions placed upon it, to maintain the peace of her patients.

Since most of the personnel at Balance Hill had been former drug addicts themselves—at least up through the nursing staff— Lola imagined that the morning nurse, given her rapid gestures, must have been a tweaker once, up on meth for days.

"Lola, we're here to help you," the nurse said as she clutched Lola's fingers.

Lola wanted to snatch them away but her body still ached with fatigue. And while the methadone IV quelled the nerve scratching emptiness left by the junk she had consumed, Lola felt relatively confident that she could not be transformed. Mamma had tried to save her when the Baptist minister threw her into the river. All that did was drive her away.

Lola wanted to pull the plug, shoot up, and be free. But Rick was paying for this and part of her didn't want to let him down. She wished he had never found her in the first place.

"How long will I be here?" Lola asked as she tried to wriggle her fingers free.

"Ah Lola, we don't put a time limit on the recovery process here. We're more interested that you heal in both body and mind, however long it takes."

"So I could be here forever? Like a retirement village?" Lola asked.

The nurse glanced at the methadone drip. "Well, not exactly." Her whisper made it sound as if she were revealing some mystery of creation. "After awhile we do need to send our wounded back into the world."

Lola figured she could go along with the program, become the perfect student, and they would release her early on good behavior. But the nurse, seemingly picking up on the notion, pushed her face closer to Lola's. Lola could detect the peppermint gum the nurse had lodged in one cheek of her mouth.

"You won't be able to fool anyone here, Lola. We've all been where you've been, every one of us. So you might as well surrender."

"Surrender what?" The words came out before Lola could stop them, since she really did not want to converse at all.

"Surrender the act," the nurse said.

For Lola, heroin marked the most potent surrender. She wanted to tell the nurse this but she calculated that it would automatically increase the time of her stay.

The nurse watched and waited.

"I don't have an act," Lola said. "Everyone has an act, sometimes many acts," the nurse said. "They are the parts we feel forced to use to get by."

Lola nodded, though she doubted that this nurse could possibly understand anything about her. The nurse had been paid to be there. None of this was real.

"Lola, I want you to think about why you're here, what you have to live for besides your next fix."

Lola tried to free her fingers. This time the nurse relented.

"I just want to be left alone," Lola said.

"Do you love anyone?" the nurse asked. Lola's mind was a fuzzy blank. With people, she never used the word love, even in her experiences with Roxy, or her afternoons with Rick.

The nurse lowered her voice. "Lola. I know about your film and about that type of expression."

Lola's back stiffened. The nurse spoke almost inaudibly now, in a whisper that sounded like a spirit was channeling through her.

"Lola, were you raped?"

"Of course not," Lola heard herself say in a distant voice that forced a confidence she did not own. Then she remembered that Balance Hill had been founded one year post Woodstock in 1970, after several hippies had OD'd.

"Haven't you ever heard of free love?" Lola asked.

Lola stared at the IV. She did not want to face the nurse directly.

The nurse took Lola's elbows and gently pushed them to the bed, which Lola took to mean "There's no escape."

"Free love was fabulous," the nurse said, unexpectedly. "When it was innocent and giving, it could be damn great."

Sensing the danger had subsided, the nurse released Lola's elbows. She leaned back, away from the bed. "But, it was more about the take and the show," the nurse said. "It was rarely giving."

The nurse lifted Lola's hand again. With her free hand, she pulled an envelope from a knapsack, which she had stashed under the bed. "These are your letters from the intervention. You might like to read them," said the nurse, and placed them beside Lola.

RECKONING

By the time Lola had awoken in Rick's band van, they were edging into Cape Cod.

"Hey beautiful," Rick said, smiling at her through the mirror up front. Lola lifted herself up from where she had been lying, slumped over in the back seat. Pain shot through her forearms so she plopped down on the vinyl again. On the third attempt she pushed herself upright, seeing flecks of colored light stream into her field of vision like meteors.

"Where are we?" Lola croaked. As she caught her gaze in his overhead mirror, she blinked. It was as though someone had punched black and blue specks around her lids.

"Massachusetts," Rick said. "I'm taking you to my mom's place, to the sea."

Lola nodded. "Thanks," she said as Rick handed her some sunglasses. She laughed. "Not my sexiest day, is it?"

He grinned but Lola could see it was not his usual smile but a forced expression. It dawned on her that he must have found her on the floor in Brooklyn, after she and the bar back had scored some junk.

She never wanted Rick to know about the dope. He always looked at her without judgment, and now she only perceived concern in his face. Lola resisted the urge to cry. If she acted casual, she could ease his worry. They could move past this.

As they pulled into the gravel driveway of the gray house with white shutters and horizontal New England shingles, Lola heard voices on the deck. They weren't alone. She had been outed.

Rick opened the back door and extended both his arms to

hoist Lola out. She thought she spotted a tear roll down one of his cheeks. She could handle his anger but tears were another thing. Men didn't cry, not the ones she had known. As she searched Rick's expression for some reassurance, he glanced sideways.

Lola allowed Rick to wrap his arms around her lower back and carry her out of the vehicle. For a minute, she considered digging for his keys and taking off in the band van. How far could she get?

Lola already knew Rick's mother from her trips to the city and she had invited Lola to visit. Rick had been planning to drive Lola to the house—which sounded like utopia when Rick explained it—but she never guessed it would happen this way.

As Rick released her, Lola leaned against the van and folded her arms across her chest.

"Loles, c'mon," he said. He looked at the ground.

Lola started to whimper. She wanted to fall on her knees before him to tell him, she wished he had never tried to find her, that it didn't seem fair. She wanted to blame him.

"Loles."

Rick rubbed away tears with both fists.

"C'mon Loles. You're my girl. Let's both get tough and go in."

Lola bit her bottom lip. The edge of her chipped tooth dug in and drew a drop of blood. Lola met the puncture with the back of her forearm to stop any flow. Rick took her free hand and led her to the front deck of the house.

Winter windows closed in the deck, and heat lamps were placed in every corner. But you could still see the ocean, a long isolated strip of beach. The waves rose several feet and crashed fiercely before rolling to the shoreline. Lola watched in silence; fantasizing about how it might feel to swim out and let the current pull her under for good.

Rick's mother approached, wearing an apron over a flannel shirt and some baggy trousers. She kissed Lola hello and placed plates on the table. She had laid out a spread on a white tablecloth: sandwiches on different breads, Caesar salad, crab salad, and a kettle of corn chowder. And around the long table, they all sat: the guitarist, bassist, drummer, keyboardist, Roxy, and Sarah.

"You two look like hell," Roxy greeted them, leaping from her place, next to Sarah.

"What the fuck is she doing here?!" Rick demanded, pointing at Sarah. He glared at Roxy. It was the first time Lola saw hate reflected in his eyes, for anyone. It filled Lola with a momentary sense of relief that maybe this whole organized session would blow up.

"Honey, it's okay," said Rick's mother. "I told Roxy it was okay."

Rick let go of Lola, which allowed her to check her coat pockets for smokes.

"What do you mean it's okay?" Rick yelled. "She's not a friend. She's press."

"Rick, calm the hell down," Roxy piped up. "Sarah's more like us than press. She knows what not to write."

When Roxy interjected, for a split second, Lola noticed Sarah wriggle in her seat. Sarah seemed more uncomfortable than she did. But then the focus shifted back to Lola. "Let's just get started," Rick's mother said. "A counselor from Balance Hill will be here any minute." Finding not one cigarette in her jacket, Lola became jittery.

Rick sat next to Lola in the middle of the table and she could sense all eyes upon her. She didn't want to connect with anyone, not even Rick.

"Anyone got a cigarette?" Lola asked. Her hands shook under the table. The bassist threw a Marlboro at her.

"Last one, Loles."

But before she could ask for a light, Rick's mother instructed, "Dig in everyone." No one touched the food, except the counselor from Balance Hill—a skinny guy with a trim gray beard—who had just arrived. He bowed hello, poured some chowder into a bowl, and then instructed everyone with letters to step forward. Roxy stood up. She placed a mahogany sculpture—wearing a neon green mini dress with a hole drilled through the middle—by her plate.

"*Lola, when I first noticed you…*" Roxy read, "*you were the coolest most intense girl on the scene. And we became best friends,*" *lovers. But now, each time you disappear, I think you might die in a corner with that shithead."*

Roxy lowered the letter and clutched the statue to her chest.

Lola wanted to tell Roxy, "Yeah, but it's fine if you supply the sex or the drugs or the food or the clothes, isn't it?"

And as if she had intercepted Lola's thoughts, Roxy dropped the sculpture into the crab salad. Sarah lifted the doll from the creamy dish, and wiping it with a linen napkin, handed it back to Roxy.

"I carved a hole where my heart would be," Roxy said. "Please take her with you to rehab. So you can remember in recovery, you will restore my heart. I love you."

Lola snatched the doll, ripped off the dress, and flung it on the table. Tears of exasperation trickled down her face as she glared at Roxy. "I would never wear that!" she hissed.

The counselor motioned Roxy to sit down. As she took her place again, Roxy drummed the edge of the table, as though she could not bear to glimpse her naked statue rejected.

Rick stood next. He pulled a folded note paper from his jacket pocket and began to read.

Loles, when you smile, the world lights up. The first time I played you a song, you were huddled in the corner of my beanbag chair. And you looked back with the eyes of a child. I wish I could save you… When I turned ten, my mother had to decide whether to save my old man or to save me from him. And she chose me, since I seemed a better bet when he was strung out. We used to find him, rolled on his side, puking his guts out on the floor next to the syringes…I never want to see you stick a needle in your arm again. It's like killing a beautiful flower at the root. Or watching the old man almost die. The high ain't worth it. It ain't worth killing beauty, which is you. And it ain't worth killing your friends, which is us…I'm here for you, Loles.

Looking up from the paper, Rick continued. "And if the old man can do it, so can you. Believe me, we never thought he'd get

who town · 164

up off the floor…Loles, get up off the floor."

Unlike Roxy, who cornered Lola's every reaction, Rick opened her up, which made her uncomfortable in a different way. If Lola cried now, she'd get up and run to the ocean. She'd bawl all the way to sea. So she laughed nervously while Rick plopped back in his seat.

The counselor clapped his hands. "So, anyone else?"

Sarah rose. As she slowly and deliberately unfolded a plain piece of paper, Lola perked up. She was curious to hear what Sarah would say, since compared to the others, she was basically a stranger. She chuckled to herself that Sarah, as press, would represent official public sentencing. It meant that Lola could be tomorrow's word on the street, "Indie Porn Star, not so glamorous now, whacked on smack, taken away in New England." Lola felt she deserved as much, but then she was surprised.

"Lola, I'm sorry," Sarah began. "*We all use you as a prop, as a scapegoat. We push you to test boundaries that scare us. We like that you shock us. The media and the publicity machines prod you with prizes and attention because your pain makes us feel safer in our own skins. But if you go any further, you'll die…And then, we're all guilty.*"

Roxy stood up and lurched forward. She shouted, "Fuck you! Fuck you Sarah!" She shoved Sarah to the ground.

The counselor jumped up to intervene. Roxy's fury had gifted Lola with a moment to escape, to run to the front of the house, across the road, anywhere. But Sarah's letter caused her to hesitate.

"You were right Rick!" Roxy screamed. "I should not have brought her. She's not a friend. She was never a friend!"

As Lola recalled the scene from her uncomfortable bed at Balance Hill, she remembered who she had been originally, before that afternoon in the hospital, when mamma told her she had become a woman. She had been called Lisa, a girl from San Antonio. Mamma had deemed her a seductive poisonous flower. Lisa had died then. Vultures had fed upon her and she resurrected as Lola.

Lola knocked the doll from her night-stand to the ground.

She read Sarah's letter again.

She would go back to being Lisa.

RELEASE

She realized, from the way that he had said "Hello Sarah" and the ensuing dead silence after she had replied "Yes" that her editor was not happy.

"Sarah, you didn't file any notes with me, or did I miss the email?" he asked.

"No, I didn't," she replied.

There was no point in concocting an excuse. She had propped herself at the tip of a spinning top, a reporting job that exhilarated her the first few rounds. But by the end she could anticipate every turn of the fantasy ride. It was only a matter of time, after she had pitched Roxy and Lola half—heartedly, before the farce stopped revolving, until she could rest.

"Sarah, you know what this means, don't you?" Sarah stood on the porch of the Cape Cod house, nodding to herself for what seemed like minutes. Finally, she spoke. "That you're letting me go."

"That's right, Sarah. it's not working. I'm sorry."

She would allow the top to fall over finally. Now, she could lift herself from beneath her editor's hand, to find a place where she didn't need to scandalize or fabricate—not only her own history—but also those solicited by the so-called *beau monde*. Each time she had lifted the paintbrush to her subjects, a finger pointed back to her, "You are as fake as they are."

"No. I'm sorry," Sarah told her editor. "I'm just not inspired by this anymore."

For a split second Sarah could almost feel his anger burning wire into cinders on the other end of the phone. He had given her the opportunity to apprentice, to eventually become like him, a first class pimp.

"I'm grateful to you. I really am," Sarah began. "You integrated me into a world that's off limits to most people. But don't you find that we're always telling the same story, over and over again?"

"Darling," he countered in a languid drawl. "It's all about illusion. And you proved too sensitive."

"This last year, only the faces changed…" Sarah replied. "Sex, drugs, and rock n'roll—unexamined sores covered or exposed as trends permit—rolled into some French garment."

Rick honked the horn of the band van. It sobered her adequately to end the conversation.

"But thank you," she said, "for the chance." And he cleared his throat, "Um, of course, Sarah. Goodbye and good luck."

Sarah clicked off her cell phone and moved toward the back seat where Rick's band sat, shoulders toppled together in mass stupor after the storm. Rick reached over to open the front door, as an exit cue to the bassist who occupied his regular co-captain post.

"Let Sarah sit up front, man."

Since Roxy had refused to give Sarah a ride back to the city in her father's limousine, Rick had offered to drive her home with his crew. Sarah climbed inside the van and sat next to Rick. The muted ammonia smell of new vinyl penetrated the air. In the summer that synthetic scent usually suffocated her senses. But hiding from the cold that day, it provided Sarah an intimate safety zone.

For the first time in her life Sarah felt light. The slumbering winter trees on either side of the house stretched out their bare branches and seemed to hold the promise of unexpected blossoms and brilliant future leaves. The open road beckoned, free of celebrity altars. And she still had Darius and their trip, ahead of her.

"You know," Rick said, interrupting her reverie. "You're not what I expected."

Sarah laughed, recognizing herself in his words.

"Oh no? What did you expect?"

"Dunno." He pulled out of the driveway. As they lumbered onto the road, he gazed over at her, from her boots to her fur collar, then her face. It was the first time Sarah could remember him looking her straight in the eye.

"I told Roxy not to let you near Lola. And yet you released her from us. You were the only one who could see what was going on, the only one who told the truth."

Rick patted her on the knee. Then realizing he had taken a physical liberty, obviously embarrassed, he yanked his hand back to the steering wheel.

"Gee thanks grandpa." Sarah said, and his shoulders shook as he began to chuckle beside her. He wasn't such an ass, after all.

A few minutes from the house, as they turned onto the highway, Sarah's mobile phone beeped, alerting her that she had a text message. It was from Darius. Excited, she clicked on it.

Hey baby. See you in Barbados in a week? Can't wait to photograph you in that thong.

Sarah blinked. It must be a mistake, a note for a model? In a few simple words, Darius had hung her feelings in a clumsily pulled noose.

The joyous anticipation of her return and subsequent escape from New York tangled her stomach in knots. Her lips trembled. She pretended to rummage for something, burying her head in her purse, so Rick could not see her tears. With her head in her lap, she wiped them abruptly away. And then the phone beeped with a second message.

Sorry, hon. Wrong number. See ya around in New York.

"Pick a CD," Rick said, as he brushed his hand lightly against her. She was glad for a distraction and reached out immediately for the CD case. As she cued up Bob Dylan's *Abandoned Love* Rick jolted back in his seat. The lyrics belted out from the front speakers:

I've been deceived by the clown inside of me
I thought that he was righteous but he's vain
I've given up the game, I've got to leave,

The pot of gold is only make believe.

Rick silently mouthed the lyrics and nodded along. A couple of guys in back rolled down the windows and flicked cigarette ashes out of them. The chill that seeped inside from the cracks seemed to rouse Rick and pull him away from the music.

"So, did Darius call?" he asked.

Sarah felt her spine tighten as though he had suddenly turned a screw. She looked at Rick anxious to hide her bleary eyes that stung and threatened to spill more tears.

Rick must have glanced at her phone screen.

"How did you?" Sarah stuttered.

Rick flashed her an apologetic half smirk. "I saw you both at the Carlyle. Was that him?"

Sarah nodded. "Yes."

Sarah would have preferred to remain a heroine in his eyes; she enjoyed the change in him, since he had recognized her. But strangely, after Darius' messages, Rick seemed to warm to her even more and patted her on the knee, again—this time, self assuredly.

"You lost nothing," Rick said. "The guy's a sex addict. But the rumor is that once he's at bat, he can't take it home. I even heard he got so ticked that he forced a bunch of guys to wear dildos."

"Really?" Sarah asked.

It all came rushing back to Sarah then, the comments Darius made about her resembling his mother, his warped Oedipal pedestal. If Rick was telling the truth, nothing real could ever be consummated between them. Darius, who proudly distorted images, was castrated by his mother. Sexual bravado proved to be the ultimate illusion.

Sarah sobbed, realizing she had nothing to hold onto. The path to nowhere and anywhere lay before her. Complete freedom prompted her to lose control, made her nerves pulse. She began to giggle. The wetness that escaped Sarah's left eye, touched Rick's palm, which still rested upon her leg. She allowed her head to remain there, for a sweet moment, as her eyelashes flitted against him.

The day after the intervention at the Cape, Sarah's dinner party story on Roxy and Lola debuted in the *Tribune*. Her byline, in bold, appeared intact, as though nothing had happened.

And Rick, who had telephoned several times to check on her, offered Sarah the band van for her drive to New Jersey. She thanked him, but she had already decided to rent a car instead, a standard Dodge.

As she pulled into a block close to the beach, Sarah considered the candy colored wooden houses, which sat side by side, ordinarily jammed with people during the summer months.

Even at the end of winter, the shore still looked the same, black speckled drifts of ivory sand, which lined mostly flat land. Unlike the Cape, the waves didn't soar ferociously but rose just slightly, then shuffled rhythmically toward resignation.

Sarah had kept Effervescent—Roxy's doll head—tucked into the bottom of her designer leather handbag. In the couple months that had passed, Sarah had almost forgotten about Effervescent, safely housed in the white box wrapped in rubber bands. And now, as she stepped out of the car and approached the beach on foot, she pulled the tiny container from her bag and unbound her captive.

"I'm freeing you," Sarah said, kissing the small wooden forehead before hurling her toward the waves.

Sarah thought about her father, who still visited the strip each summer with her mother. She remembered their shell collections, painstakingly selected. But, as Sarah walked back to the car, she noticed that for every perfect shell—smooth alabaster, pearl gray, black and ridged—there were thousands of broken shells. Shards of different varieties amassed together, collapsed on top of one another. They glittered from different angles, depending on how and when the sun struck. And from a distance, they resembled jewels.

Modern Cult of Intellect: Special to the Tribune By Sarah Rosen

"I could just eat her up," said sculptor Roxy Sullivan about her friend and part time lover, Lola Fanuk, the actress who starred in *Le Sexe, Je Veux, Je Ne Veux Pas* directed by Jarrett K. The film—rated X—had been released cinematically in France but banned in the United States. Ms. Fanuk was lounging on a red-fringed pillow, her legs crossed Indian style. Her strawberry blonde curls grazed her skinny shoulders, which peered out like knobs from a sleeveless silver Gucci tank.

"C'est l'erotique sensible," the French called Ms. Fanuk's character—sensitive eroticism. While the Americans just called it pretentious.

"Lola's so brave about her roles," said Ms. Sullivan, who had tied her red and platinum striped hair back into a short tail of sprouting threads as she chopped celery for Sunday dinner at her Tribeca loft.

As Ms. Sullivan slammed the knife on the board, she nodded towards Ms. Fanuk's pillow seat. "She's not afraid to show her humanity and often times that means baring her body."

So one might imagine that among sympathetic friends like Ms. Sullivan, Ms. Fanuk could drop her role of cinematic courtesan. But it seemed more likely as the guests arrived at Ms. Sullivan's monthly supper parties, that even more roles were cast.

The ensuing scene bore little resemblance to Dorothy Parker's politically minded artists' coalition at the Algonquin in the Fifties; or even Andy Warhol's vivacious Factory of the Eighties, replete with whip dancers and silver lamé. But the crowd represented a cross section of those who currently influence taste throughout the globe: Rick Five, a guitarist, the son of Seventies icon, Mick Five, a bar man from Williamsburg, who was a male companion of Ms. Fanuk, a tee shirt designer who combs big cities for the latest graffiti innovations, a novelist who just released his first book *Punk Anthology X* (Radical Press), and a model and "It girl."

Ms. Sullivan herself, a Connecticut native and socialite, is known to create wooden images often based upon herself. These tiny depictions, each barely six inches high, of carved mahogany, popped up in the most unusual places, copping various angles—climbing pillows on all fours and asserting their stick arms upward within wall corners. Two were placed catty corner, so that if the observer were to blink, they appeared to practically claw the silver buttons of the CD player. Ms. Sullivan's statues had no boundaries.

Ms. Fanuk chuckled. "Roxy's sculptures maintain a busy social calendar, like their mom."

Aside from the art figurines, the live guests sat in a circle on gold threaded Moroccan pillows that Ms. Sullivan had purchased on a family voyage to Tunisia.

As Buddhist chants—favorite tracks of Ms. Sullivan—played on the stereo, they all fed upon vegan spinach dumplings and each other's current proclivities.

"I am still a big fan of synthesizer groups," said Ms. Fanuk. "It's how all the electro clash music is derived. The originals were totally underrated in the Eighties. No one seems to honor the happy music, which is about embracing life. And continuous arousal."

"I'd like to write an anthology of new wave next, to examine the impact of the synthesizer on human emotion," the novelist told the *Tribune*. "It had the opposite effect to punk."

"That music has inspired me," said the tee shirt designer. "Neon logos are analogous to synth. It's open minded. The possibilities are endless."

Mr. Five, whose corkscrew ink colored hair was tied back into a rubber band, placed himself off to the side of the circle.

He forewent a cushion to sit cross-legged on a square of the hard wood planks not flanked by oriental rugs. Mr. Five's father is deemed one of the greatest metal guitarists of all time. When the *Tribune* asked Mr. Five the younger how new wave fit into rock and roll, he shrugged. "It's all derivative. Nothing's new. And the current stuff's just processed and canned."

Ms. Sullivan served her signature vegetarian stir-fry, ordered straight from Thai Fantasy catering. She was careful when lifting the china as not to splatter her indigo Rockla jeans or Christian Dior peacock feathered top. This garnered admiration from the model, who mentioned that Louis Viutton would debut a similar peacock print, in an evening bag at the end of this month.

Ms. Fanuk stood, smoothing the shiny round sequins of her tank with one hand while lifting her glass of Veuve Clicquot with the other. She had recommended champagne to Ms. Sullivan, suggesting, "The sweet bubbly opposes the coriander spice."

She initiated the communal clink of Baccarat flutes.

"Time to turn on," she said.